Mullins Collection of Best New Fiction

EDITED BY AARON MULLINS

ISBN: 9781797422237

FOREWORD

You never know where a good tale is going to lead you, but imagine for a moment that the beginning was also unknown. Like a book without a cover. Experience the mystery and excitement of exploring a world populated with creatures unlike any you have ever seen, ghouls that feed in the darkness of the London underground in The Orphaned City and the strange patient who stalks the halls of a mental asylum in Inferiority Complex. Then discover worlds where humans themselves are the most curious species of all, the charming smile of the mysterious Jack in Knowing Jack and the devious mind of Red in The Path I Set Upon.

Travel between worlds bound together by one all encompassing weave of storytelling. Fiction has the ability to create these new worlds, which still reflect our lives in the real world. Each story in this collection offers a different perspective on human experience, a glimpse of who we really are, who we might have been, or who we wish to become. Will the next story scare you, or make you think differently about the world? Will it spark into life a new idea, the kind that Jake develops from an overheard conversation in Dreamworld. Or question our very existence, like the revelations of Professor Westerham in Reflection. It might even lead to a dangerous hunt for untold riches, which Ryan experiences in The Hassam Legacy.

Whatever your tastes, this book holds a story for everyone. You may even discover a love for stories you wouldn't have considered before. Fiction does that to you. It draws you into its welcoming embrace. Sometimes the welcome is warm, like the strength of Helen after dealing with death in Coming of Age. Other times you feel an icy chill as the story grips you, like the terror that claws at Meg when she hears her parrot speak in Scared to Death. Either way, you'll always remember how you felt when you took your first step.

So take that step now. Discover a collection of stories linked, not by genre, but by their ability to make you think and feel. Nine different worlds are waiting to be explored. Each hides a secret, a twist that awaits discovery by an adventurous reader.

Welcome to our worlds.

Aaron Mullins

www.aaronmullins.com

CONTENTS

DEDICATION

When you believe in each other, anything is possible.
This book is for the doers, achievers and believers.
And those who appreciate their work.

BY AARON MULLINS

FICTION
Mullins Collection of Best New Fiction
Mullins Collection of Best New Horror

WRITING GUIDES
How to Write Fiction: A Creative Writing Guide

BUSINESS GUIDES
How to Write a Business Plan
The Ultimate Business Plan Template

PSYCHOLOGY: ACADEMIC
Ethnic Differences in Perceptions of Social Responsibility
Risk Perception in Extreme Event Decision Making
The Effect of Mate Value on Self-esteem
The Impact of Social Responsibility on Community Resilience
Enhancing Community Resilience to Flooding
Flood Hazards: Impacts and Responses (chapter)
Social Responsibility and Community Resilience: a Definition, Context and Methodology

www.aaronmullins.com

1. REFLECTION

Alan Peabody

Aliens are not travellers from outer space, as many suppose. They are time travellers from our own future. I know that this is a populist theory, but I can say it with absolute conviction because David, who had the finest mind I have ever encountered, discovered the secret of time travel. It was subsequently proved to me beyond all doubt because I met one of them and she became a dear friend. If you pause to think about it, then it is the most rational explanation. The chances of another life form being created in the universe, in our own time, that is sufficiently similar to ours that there would be the slightest thing in common, is a lot slimmer than the chances of time travel being impossible, which as I say, it is not.

*

I sat back and took a breath. I had just read the first paragraph from a file of papers I had discovered in my mother's effects. My mother was Lindsay Shawbridge. I expect you've heard of her, if not as Lindsay Shawbridge, under which name she wrote two well respected biographies, then as J Ralph Terling, the science fiction author. She had died a couple of months ago and I had just begun to sort through her papers.

If I am honest, and I may as well be, my interest overcame my grief quite easily. It didn't dispose of the grief, which was still raw, it just nudged it aside. My mother was, after all, a very interesting person.

This particular folder was in a box marked 'papers from C Westerham', a name I instantly recognised. Sir Charles Westerham, Wykeham Emeritus Professor of Physics at Oxford University, was the subject of her first biography. Nobel Prize winner and the head of sub atomic particle research at the Rutherford Appleton Laboratory when he died, thirty some years ago in 1978. She had been a student of his and had been given extensive access to his papers. It made her quietly famous, I suppose.

I took a sip from my cup of tea and read on.

*

It all started the day David entered my rooms, quietly as I was giving a tutorial to my 'select' group. I had invited him and today he was late, which was unusual. In those days I was a lecturer in the then relatively young science of atomic physics and I offered additional tutorials to promising students. Five years earlier David had been one such student. Now he was on my research staff. Already I knew he would go places I wouldn't ever be able to. If only I had known just how far. Tuesday, August 26th 1955. I'll never forget that day.

David leaned back on the window sill and waited. I could see that he was almost bursting to talk to me. Once or twice he contributed to the discussion, but his mind was elsewhere. Eventually the tutorial ended and the group left.

'Come on then. Let's have it,' I said.

'Neutrinos can travel through time,' he announced.

To say I was doubtful was putting it mildly. Neutrinos were a theoretical postulate in those days, but David said he had detected them in the reactor at Windscale and he found some strange effects in their behaviour. He had been corresponding with some Americans, Cowan and Reines. Historically they were credited with the detection of the neutrino over a year after David had done it; his own priorities having changed.

He moved to the blackboard and began to explain. It was a long discussion. We returned to that board many times over the next weeks. I had to relocate my tutorials so that it couldn't be wiped. Eventually I took to photographing it. The detection proof was sound and I urged him to establish his results and publish. But he was set on this unexplained anomaly which he said showed that the neutrinos had arrived before they left.

'Can't you see it, Charles? If a particle arrives before it has left then we can see into the future.'

'And the past,' I added wryly. 'But David, you have simply chosen an explanation for a measurement anomaly. It could just be a calibration error, however careful you have been. Besides I'm sure there is a more rational explanation. We can't just chuck Einstein out of the window, the poor man's been dead less than a year.'

My clumsy attempt at humour fell flat. 'OK, Charles,' He said. 'I'll bring you some practical proof. I may be a while though.'

Things returned to normal. The Americans ultimately managed their neutrino detection and claimed the glory that would otherwise have been David's, with perhaps a small mention for me I suppose. He never referred to it, or to his proposal that neutrinos travelled through time. He behaved precisely as normal, except that every once in a while I would hear that he had borrowed some piece of equipment or other and that it was a long time coming back.

Somewhat over a year later I was battling the Telegraph Crossword. Six down was a real stinker and I just couldn't get it. Completing the crossword before nine o'clock was a matter of pride and I rarely failed. David entered and poured himself a cup of tea from the pot. He looked over my shoulder and said. 'Yes, that's a hard one isn't it?'

'It is. Diablo is certainly being the devil today.' Diablo was the setter and always made six down hard. Then David nonchalantly told me the answer. And it was right. You can always see these things once you know. Cunning clue.

'I didn't think you did the crossword?' I said.

'I don't,' he replied. 'I can't get the hang of it.'

'Penny just dropped on this one, eh?'

'No. I read the answer in tomorrow's paper.'

I laughed.

'You asked for proof, I've just brought you some,' he said deadpan.

It was a moment before I remembered his neutrino time travel theory.

'David, you're a scientist. You know this isn't proof of anything, you need mathematical rigor, you need results.' I was beginning to splutter.

Then he laughed too. 'I had you going there for a moment, didn't I? Yes, I just saw the answer and took my chance. Quick thinking eh? Anyway, look, can you meet me in The Chequers for lunch. There's someone I'd like you to meet.'

Knowing what I do now, I would say that that day was the one where things entered phase two.

He knew my timetable well and had chosen a good day. I had the afternoon clear until around three. I arrived at the old pub and he met me almost at the door and took me to a table he had secured. Seated at the table there was the finest looking young woman I had ever seen. It wasn't that she was beautiful, although she was in a classical sense. It was simply that she was apparently a perfect physical specimen, simply exuding good health in a way you rarely saw.

'Charles. I should like you to meet Siobhan. We're going to be married.'

Bombs had orphaned David in the war and his older brother had been killed in Normandy. The university was now his family and I, if you like, was his uncle. So this was an important moment and I did my best. She was a lovely girl, but I couldn't place her accent. In those days there were still people coming in from Europe, which remained in a dreadful mess. So one didn't pry. When I asked where she was from and she just replied, 'Oh, here and there.' I left it at that. Her English was absolutely perfect but I couldn't place that accent.

True young love is a rare thing and I have to confess, it is something I had never experienced myself, but they had it. They were young and deeply in love. Oh, I was married and had children. I loved them all, my wife too. But I was never in love like they were. Mine was a very English sort of marriage, an Oxford kind of affair. Now, as I reach my very old age, I am past most regrets. But David and Siobhan had true love, something I should have liked to have. Perhaps I did find true love eventually, but I was older.

In fact they never did marry. I think they just couldn't be bothered with it all. Certainly they lived their lives together as though they were married. In those days it was not as uncommon as one might suppose, couples just living together. Apart from the odd prudish look from one or another of the wives, no-one bothered. She became his partner in research, as well as in life. Where he was prone to brilliant flashes of insight, she was methodical and systematic. She probed all the corners of his ideas until there were no unanswered questions. Their work was outstanding and I confess the foundation for some of my own published theories. I haven't stolen their work. Siobhan said I was welcome to it all, with certain provisos. As to those, I'll come to them later.

Two years passed and they published a paper on subatomic interactions and a few small corrections to Pauli's neutrino postulations, which were well received and got them a grant for further research spending. This took them out of Oxford, but we stayed in close touch even so. Over time they became my dearest friends. I think, on reflection, that I may have been a little in love with Siobhan myself. Their research had to be conducted using a nuclear reactor and we didn't have one at Oxford, of course. It's a long way to the sea.

One evening in 1961 I was staying in my rooms, something I increasingly did in those days, when Siobhan came to see me. She was by herself and she had come, she said, to explain a few things and to say goodbye.

This was rather sudden. I assumed that they had an offer to take their research to America, so many did around that time. So naturally I asked where they were going and where David was. In fact I was full of questions, but she forestalled me, telling me that she would explain it all, but that it was going to be a long night and that we might need coffee. Without waiting she went to my little kitchen and made some.

The first thing was that she was going to have a baby. I was overjoyed for them, but she said that was the main reason they had to go.

'Surely not. If it's those stupid prudes, then put on a ring,' I said. But she said that wasn't it and things were more complicated than that. The day was always coming when they would have to go. She was an alien. By which she meant that she was from the future, a little over four hundred years.

She took the trouble to prove that to me, although I was rather unconvinced until after they had left. There were no visitors from other planets that she was aware of. There was reconnaissance and other visits from the future, which had given rise to the alien stories. Due to the risks of time travel altering the past, which is entirely possible incidentally as each person has their own time frame, it had become rigidly controlled and inevitably, as is the way of governments, a tool of oppression.

Initially observers were sent back in time to ensure that things that were supposed to happen, happened as they were supposed to. Then as government became less democratic, they tightened their grip. Agents were sent back to make carefully calculated changes to enable the government to maintain a tighter grip on power. Siobhan was one such agent sent back in time. Her official mission was to ensure that David did discover the neutrino time travel effect, which is true by the way. One day someone may stumble on it. She was a double agent though. She belonged to an ancient movement that held to the belief that meddling was wrong and that life on the planet should take its natural course. In time they had become a kind of secret society. For years they had been trying to infiltrate the government operation and it was a remarkable achievement that she herself got into the position that she was sent back to ensure David made his discovery, only to intend quite the opposite effect.

She had arrived just a couple of days after David had his first insights and had taken time to get to know him, rather than leap straight in and begin to disrupt his work. She couldn't stop his mind working. Initially she had pushed him to create just a time viewer, in the hope that would satisfy him. He was never any good with crosswords, she added and really had read that six down answer in the next day's paper, having seen me struggle with that clue in the viewer from a couple of days earlier. He couldn't resist teasing me a little. But he saw the possibility for physical time travel straight away.

The plan had been to kill him if that happened, she said, and hang the consequences.

But she loved him. Instead she told him everything. Since then they had been together working on their escape machine. She knew the principles of time travel, of course, it was part of general science knowledge in her time. With David's insight they had solved it. And really just in the nick of time because she had become pregnant. Having a baby in her own past carried incalculable consequences, and so they were leaving. They had to at some point. David had wanted to come to say goodbye, but there was just too much to do. Every moment they delayed increased the risk for the baby.

They were going in the next day or two, as soon as the conditions in the reactor were right. They would leave no trace of their work as they hoped that the secret would leave with them.

Of course this was short in the telling, but all night in the convincing and she was right that we needed the coffee. Then she kissed me and left. I never saw them again. I heard from them, in a manner of speaking. The experimental reactor where they worked on the Kent coast simply stopped. There was no explosion, no fire, nothing. Just stone cold, no atomic reaction, no radiation. A lump of lead. It was like all the energy had been sucked out of it, which it had been. I was sent to investigate, the ideal choice as it happened. Of course the police were also investigating the disappearance of David and Siobhan. But there was no link to establish. Both things remained a mystery, a rather expensive one in the case of the reactor, but I chose to not explain either of them.

Naturally there was my own curiosity. I had my photographs from those early blackboard days and knowing for certain that something is possible is a great encouragement. Armed with the knowledge that it is possible, I was able to work it out for myself. But that is a far as I took the matter. It was David and Siobhan's intention that it remain undiscovered and that's the way it is. My notes are hidden away. One day someone else may independently stumble on the secrets I hide, but a mind like David's is rare.

I don't know what kind of society they returned to, but it seems to me that it should be better than the one she left. Or maybe they just went on further into the future. As the secret of time travel is hidden, I never will know. Now, as I reach the end of my days I care more about our legacy, even if, in this case, the legacy is to a distant future.

I have written this for my remaining dearest friend, who I know will treat it with care. She has been the best thing about my later life. By this time she will know that I have lost the fight with my failing cells as they multiply insidiously within me. And so I will get myself to the post box and then return to swallow the two yellow tablets my friend from the medical school has kindly provided. I have no desire for screaming pain and I am satisfied with my life.

Time catches up with us all.

*

I leaned back in my chair and took a long deep breath. But there was more. My mother had appended one more page. Just a brief few words, but enough to reduce me to helpless tears.

*

My Dear Siobhan,

If you are reading this then I must be gone. If you haven't yet realised, I named you for her. It was your father's wish. I never told you about your father. He was a very special man and many years older than me when we met. The university would never have tolerated it, had it been made public, even then, and really all his wife had was the reflected glory of his achievements. He wasn't cruel and wouldn't destroy her. Also, being honest, his work was his life. So we kept the affair quiet. Only we two knew and as I was his biographer it was never likely to come out.

He wanted to preserve the knowledge and protect the secret, in case it should ever be needed, and so I am passing it on to you. Both the secret and the location of the knowledge. They have recently discovered the neutrino time jump effect using billions of dollars and a hole in a mountain, although for now they think it is something else. David and your father managed it with much less and a long time ago. So the discovery may come. If it does then I beg you to use the knowledge to stop it becoming a tool of oppression if you can. They would have wanted that.

At home, 10 December 2011

2. DREAMWORLD

Stephen Terry

'If Nicole's begging for mercy, she doesn't deserve it,' said the woman. 'Fact is, Bryn, she'd quite happily snuff you if it was her doing the killing. That's the criminal mindset.'

Jake swallowed his Theakston's and tried to read the week-end edition of the Evening Herald, while half listening to the couple at the next table. Probably some out of work actors, practicing for a West-End role. The pub was a haunt for them.

'So that makes it easier then,' the man replied. 'She might be the daughter of MacBride, but she's our hostage, Tora.'

'She's a murderer,' the woman said. 'You know that's what we had to do?'

'Yeah, well, fingers and all that…'

'Just cool it,' she said. 'Keep your voice down. Get another beer if you want.'

'You want one?'

'Diet Coke.'

'With ice?'

'Just get the drinks. Put a Bacardi in it. Make it a large one.'

Jake's mobile phone vibrated. Incoming SMS. He adjusted his reading glasses. 'Staying with Sheila for week-end. Little one sleeping. Miss you. XXX Emmy.'

'Be good. Take care. XXX Jake.' He clicked the send button. The pregnancy had been difficult; her hormones were all over the place. 'Bloody boring bookworm,' she had taunted. 'What sort of father you going to be, living in a dream world half the time?'

He resented that. Dream worlds could be exciting places. He would sit the little one on his knee and he would be the hero, a Harrison Ford, a Johnny Depp or even a Harry Potter. He would slay wicked witches and rescue damsels in distress. The little one would love to listen to her hero. He smiled to himself and picked up the Londoner's menu. When the waitress passed by with a few empty glasses, he beckoned her over to order a cheese toasty and another drink. Then he started the crossword.

'Bryn you've had enough, time to go,' said the woman. 'We're out of here pronto, or we'll miss the train. Get the bags, while I flag down a cab.' Jake watched them go. He finished the crossword and glanced over at their table. A jiffy bag was on the floor under her seat. He frowned, reached across and picked it up. He jumped up and ran to the pub door and opened it. Rain spat at him. Too late, they had gone and it was time he went too. He tucked the jiffy bag into his raincoat, opened his umbrella and stepped outside.

Martin MacBride was the name on the jiffy bag. Sanford House, Teddington, London TW11 3HS. Inside was a disc. On the front was a label. 'Nicole.' Nearly midnight, but he was intrigued. Jake put it into the DVD player and switched it on. He wished he hadn't.

He just made it to the bathroom. The film flickered through his head frame by frame. 'Nicole' was naked and tied to a marble table begging for mercy. The hooded person - he couldn't tell if it was male or female - was holding a pair of secateurs and a metal bowl. Nicole screamed and sobbed as a finger was severed. Fresh blood dripped from the stump. The person showed the contents of the bowl to the camera. The secateurs then caressed Nicole's nipples. The message was clear.

*

Nicole heard the clatter of feet coming down the stone steps of the cellar. Both of them. She cringed. It wasn't food and water. Only the man would bring that. He would do things to her and, if she complied with his demands, he would turn on the electric fire while he used a fork and a spoon to feed her and gave her water from a plastic bottle. 'You've been a good girl, today' he would say if she pleased him. She shuddered as the light came on.

'Nicole, time for another photo-shoot,' said the woman. 'Your Daddy will be pleased to see his little girl.'

She begged for mercy when the camera started, and screamed when the secateurs closed around her little toe. It plopped into the metal bowl. The camera zoomed in for a close-up.

'Haven't you finished it yet?' complained the woman.

'I'm making a copy, just in case,' he replied. Wrong answer.

'In case of what?' Her voice rising sharply. 'You going to lose another one, or maybe give it to Inspector Morse?'

'She's just a girl, it makes me sick thinking about what we're doing to her.'

The woman laughed. 'Bloody hypocrite. Listen up. She's a murderer. I don't care if we've got to cut off every last bit, that'll be too good for the bitch. I want to see MacBride begging for his precious little daughter's life. And don't think I don't know about your cosy chats, the room stinks of male excretions.'

Afterwards, when the woman had gone, the man bandaged her foot and cleaned up the mess. He helped her with the toilet pan and gave her some more pain-killers. The fight had gone and she just lay there shivering and moaning. He seemed concerned. 'Is my little girl cold?' he said.

'Please don't hurt me anymore,' she pleaded. 'I'll give you anything you want, just let me go.'

He smiled at her. 'Is my baby going to be a good girl, then?'

*

Jake thought it through. He could just forget it and no-one would be any wiser. Not an option. Nicole's terror was real. She needed help. He could go to the police. Who was Martin MacBride? Was he being blackmailed, or was he a client of some snuff ring? If that was the case, would Jake be in any danger? No answers, just questions. Any other clues?

He retrieved the DVD and examined it. No identifying marks, just a bog standard Re-Write disc that could be bought from any high street store. The bag, though, had Richmond upon Thames Post Office embossed on the back flap under the seal. Narrowed the field to two hundred thousand residents or so. Martin MacBride and the couple could have been neighbours. Interesting concept. Well, he had the whole week-end, since Emmy was away. The only factual clue he had was the address. First stop then, Mr. MacBride.

*

There was a high wall surrounding the grounds and a guard stood by the main gate with an Alsatian growling at his side. The man mountain waved impatiently at Jake as he pedaled up the lane to the gate.

'Private property, son, didn't you just see the sign. Now just backtrack up to the main road, or my dog will give you a taste.'

Friendly sort. They liked their privacy undisturbed that was for sure.

'Look it's important I see Mr. MacBride,' he said.

'Yer man doesn't live here. Now feck-off.'

'Tell him it's about Nicole.'

The man grunted something incomprehensible and called someone on his cell phone. Jake waited.

'Follow the drive. Any fecking funny business, son, and you'll be dealing with me, okay?'

Jake nodded, adjusted his helmet, and rode the BMX through the gates and up to the house.

The grey haired man had piercing blue eyes and spoke with a soft Irish accent. 'We are wary of blow-in strangers, there're those that'll steal the shirt from your back and there's always The Troubles.' He frowned and looked upwards as if remembering darker times. He took Jake by the arm. 'What's your name son, and what is it you want from me? My man Gregor tells me you know my daughter… would I be hearing him correct?'

'Mr. MacBride, I'm Jake, and there's something you need to see.' Jake gave him the DVD. 'The girl in the film is being tortured.'

'Better we see for ourselves then,' he said in a quiet voice, as if pain and suffering was a cross to bear. Perhaps it was. He led Jake to a room and pointed to the seats.

'Take the weight off your legs.'

Jake looked around. Austere, a picture of the Virgin Mary on the wall. Tiled floor supporting a coffee table and a black leather sofa with two matching chairs. TV and DVD player resting on a small wooden cabinet. He chose one of the chairs and stifled his nausea as MacBride started the film.

He played it through twice. Afterwards, he turned to Jake. 'Have you told anyone else, or spoken to the police?'

Jake shook his head. 'Not yet. Nobody else has seen it. I figured you would know what to do.'

The man couldn't have phrased it better. 'You're a good man yourself, but you shouldn't have got mixed up in this,' he said. 'It's private business.' He got up and ejected the DVD and put it on the coffee table. 'Now what are we going to do about you?'

He looked like a vulture about to descend on its prey. Beads of sweat broke out on Jake's forehead, his breath quickened and he felt even more uneasy when MacBride phoned Gregor.

*

'Can you shoot a gun, son?' asked Martin. Jake nodded slowly. His father, cast from the Hemingway mould, had enrolled him into a West London shooting school when he was a teenager. For a while he could be a James Bond, a Tom Cruise or, even better, a Jason Bourne, but he lost interest when his father died in a shooting accident on the Scottish Moors.

The gun, lying in a cellophane bag on the table and used by Military and Police agencies, was a Smith & Wesson M&P 9mm pistol. Next to the gun were the contents of Jake's pockets and photos of Emmy and the baby. Gregor had been thorough.

Martin put on a paternal look. 'Thing is Jake, we know who you are. You have a wife and a little baby girl. We know where you live and work.' He picked up Jake's ID card. 'Librarian is a good trade. Shaw's a forgivable sin. If only he was Catholic he'd be revered. You read any of his work?'

'What do you want from me?' Jake's stomach churned.

'Retribution. We know who they are. It is time to end it.'

Jake was puzzled. 'Why not go to the police?'

Martin spat into his hand. 'The police will not be involved,' he said. 'This justice is personal, but I cannot be connected at all.'

Jake's voice rose. 'You expect me to shoot two people and rescue Nicole, you're crazy. It's impossible. No way.'

Martin pointed out of the window. 'We have a pig sty in our orchard. It's not large, but sufficient for our needs. Pigs will eat anything and everything. There will be no trace.' Jake felt cold sweat running down his spine. Martin continued, 'Gregor can show you, if you like.' He sank back into the sofa and waited.

'Blackmail,' said Jake, his whole body trembling in anger and fear.

'That would be about right, my son. Blackmail it is. You know too much. Desperate measures.'

'And if I do what you want?'

'You'll be seeing your daughter growing up.'

'And if I go to the police?'

Martin scoffed. 'Come here. What have you got? An untraceable gun, a fairy story. Nicole would die if the police were involved, that's no blarney. And you can't hide from us.' He picked up the gun and offered it.

Jake felt a blackness descend, his nightmare. He took hold of the gun, hoping that Martin would relent, but he didn't.

'Bryn and Tora Wilcox live in an old Victorian house along the Kew road. There's more than enough shrubbery to give you cover. There's a cellar off the kitchen at the back of the house, they'll keep Nicole there.' He gave Jake the address and looked at his watch. 'It's past the time you should be making a move, son, while it's still light… and I mean what I say. If you value your daughter's life, don't go bringing the police round here.'

*

Nicole felt the bump on her head with her bandaged hand. It still hurt. They must have watched the house for days, maybe weeks. It was so stupid of her to walk down the lane alone. Back from night school, she didn't see who had hit her.

It would have to be the man. No choice really, he was the one who washed her, fed her, and abused her. If she could get him to untie her, she would have a chance. If he wore his hood, his sight would be hampered, and she would use whatever she could grip to disable him. She waited for the sound of his footsteps. It would be soon.

She shivered in the gloom, heard the condensation dripping off the cold stone walls onto the concrete floor. They weren't going to release her, were they? They wanted revenge. She had to escape somehow.

If she said she'd do it, he'd offer to untie her hand. Gain his confidence, she thought. Don't rush; one hand at a time. She laughed inwardly at her macabre joke. But it had a malevolent edge. Next time she would encourage him further until she could reach the fork.

She heard him coming down the cellar stairs. Was it food time already? She had lost track of time. He opened the door, moved over to her and put the dinner tray on the bedside table. He whispered. 'She wants another photo shoot later, Nicole.'

Nicole sobbed, her chest heaving. He watched her breasts.

'There, there baby, Daddy will take care.' He sounded concerned.

'Can I hug you Daddy?' she replied between sobs. 'And touch you where you like it.'

'OK, baby,' he said, untying her hands and releasing her legs. She saw him unzipping his trousers, pulling down his jockey shorts and exposing himself. She sat up and patted the bed beside her. As he lay down she reached up and grabbed the fork, and with a cry of rage she thrust it deep into his groin, twisting and goring into his flesh.

He screamed and stared at the dark blood pumping from the wound. Femoral artery. Panicking, he tried to stem the flow, but she fought him, jabbing at his hooded eyes with the fork. 'No please don't,' he begged. 'Don't hurt me, please Nicole, it wasn't my idea to…' At the end he glared disbelievingly at his sodden genitals. Nicole watched him look up at a shadow. Maybe he saw a dark spectre beckoning him to the underworld.

*

The kitchen door was open. Jake saw the cellar light and heard screams of pain. He gritted his teeth and, holding the gun in front of him, descended the stairs into a bloody hell. The woman was slashing wildly at the girl with a knife. Nicole and Tora. Fresh blood streamed down Nicole's face. Tora was screaming incoherently as Nicole tried to avoid the blade.

He briefly closed his eyes. Upon opening them again he saw the man lying in a pool of blood on a marble table. No movement, nothing. His eyes were staring into space.

Jake fired a shot into the women's leg. She staggered and spun around. The knife clattered to the floor.

'Get away from her,' he shouted, the adrenalin kicking in hard. 'Now, or you're dead.'

She dropped to her knees as Jake took careful aim. His finger tightened on the trigger.

Retribution, it is time to end it.

The women held up an arm. 'Wait,' she pleaded. Her eyes filled with tears as she begged for mercy. The words gabbled out. 'You don't understand. She - killed - our - baby. Our little girl, Josephine. No-one believed us, especially not her precious Father.' She reached out to touch the dead man's leg. 'Now she has murdered my husband. Both gone. I have no-one. No-one.' The dam broke. All the pent up pain. She wrapped her arms around herself, rocking and weeping.

Jake hesitated and looked questioningly at the young girl staring in wide eyed shock. 'Babysitting,' she mumbled in a mono tone. 'First time. I didn't know what to do.' Anguish showed on her face. 'The baby wouldn't stop bawling. I couldn't hear the TV. The pillow, it was so peaceful, like a dream.' She started to move away from the gun. 'I didn't mean to hurt her, only send her to sleep, it was an acc...' Her voice trailed off as he took aim. Jake pulled the trigger.

Jake pedaled along the road, not believing what he had done.
Murderer.

It was horrendous. He cycled past a graveyard, the headstones grey and menacing. He looked up and focused on the name plate. St Nicholas. This was it. Sanctuary. No-one could touch him there. The church door beckoned and he found it was unlocked. He went inside. The priest was on his knees. Jake moved up close. 'Father,' he mumbled.

'...Holy Mary, mother of God, pray for us sinners now and at the hour of our death. Amen.' The priest finished his prayer and got to his feet. The blue eyes pierced into Jake's soul. 'You'll be wanting confession then,' said Reverend Martin MacBride.

3. THE PATH I SET UPON

Sophie Jonas-Hill

The house had something American Gothic about it, though nothing it minded to share. It was wreathed in bougainvillea and anticipation, and it watched me. There should have been a rocker on the front porch, a screen door and an old dog with a grey muzzle, but there was not. The large front windows regarded me with the air of one unused to guests and reluctant to break with custom.

I stumbled forward, put out my hand and caught hold of the fence that straggled across the front yard. I was hot, dizzy, my head pounded as if there were something trapped inside. I couldn't remember how long I'd been walking, where I'd walked from or who I was. I needed to sleep like I needed to breath, but the house did not want me.

You're just gonna have to get over yourself, I told it.

I walked up the pea grit path, watching my feet in their worn canvas pumps, the impression of toes worked into the blue fabric. The air was still, the heartbeat of the day slow and languid. The shadow of the house brought the scent of the blooms and the sigh and crack of the swamp. The first step creaked, the second moaned like something disappointed, and my hand secured the wooden pillar at the top of the stairs.

The front door was open, just like the good old days. I ached for something to ground this reality, but there was only the house, the road drawing a line in the dust against the dank expanse of water and stunted trees.

I focused on the small wooden veranda, with dusty boots abandoned at the door. I clung to the pillar as heat, sweat and nausea threatened to rise up and drag me down, my mouth as cracked and dry, as if I was made of the road and had travelled as far to get here. I saw a movement inside.

'Hey there.' With movement came a voice, deep, dry and lit with apprehension.

'Hello?' My voice was worn to a thread by the buzz and hum of the day. A man formed from the shadows, squinted into the light; shading his eyes with his hand. I blinked away painful tears.

'You...' he paused at the threshold; I saw a taut, hard face almost triangular in shape, faded jeans and white shirt. 'Mercy,' he said, as something dark and glittery seeped into my vision, 'what on God's green earth-'

'I'm sorry,' I interrupted, sagging against the pillar, 'I'm sorry to bother you but...' he took hold of me all in a rush, seeing I was losing my grip on pillar and on reality, 'I'm lost.' I said, into a face crosshatched with confusion.

'Why, you're a long way from home, just a moment, if you'll forgive,' he caught hold of me, 'but I'm gonna needs take a hold on you.' He maneuvered us both inside.

The place was dark but not cool; the heat of the day had soaked it through to the skin.

'Now, now... you just hold on a while, let me get you so as you can sit yourself... there.' I was aware of a wooden floor, square utilitarian furniture and one grey couch, which he lowered me onto. I bent and pain ripped through my side; I yelped as much as my parched voice and pounding head would allow.

'Did I...' he started a little, and seemed to look at me with almost professional attention. 'Well, look at that - what did you say your name was?'

'I... I can't remember, I'm sorry.' I clutched at his hand as throbbing shook my body.

'Really?' He tilted his head, one eyebrow arched. 'How... unfortunate. Well,' he looked down again, 'whoever you are, miss, you seem to be sorely afflicted - begging your indulgence but might I take a look?' I couldn't hold myself and collapsed against the couch.

'Sure.' Anything, I thought, just give me a drink.

'Now don't you mind me but I'm 'fraid this might sting a little,' he peeled back my t-shirt and the sting kicked like a mule. He grinned sheepishly, 'do forgive me for causing such distress, but this looks like a bullet wound.' His tongue flickered across his lips for a moment. 'And you say you've no memory of how you came by this, or indeed the substantial...' he indicated his forehead with spidery white fingers 'blow to your head?'

I raised my hand, encountering swelling and pain. 'No... shit.' I frowned and it hurt. It hurt even more to remember, staring into a whistling black void with a red ache hammering at the back of my eyes. 'I'm so sorry.'

'No need to apologise.' He ran his hand through his hair, a little of which sprang up again at his temples. 'Seems as how you're the victim of some sort of incident…' his voice trailed off, lazy and languid as the day outside. God, he spoke like he'd been baptized in the bayou and raised on syrup and sunshine - 'perhaps the victim of some sort of carjacking, as the modern parlance has is, judging by the mess of them pumps and the lack of any other transportation.' I could have eaten that voice off a spoon.

He stood up, 'Seems to me as that I needs try fix you up a little-'

'You a doctor?' I almost smiled, lulled by pain and the mesmerising lilt of his voice.

He chuckled, 'bless you no, but I done my time serving God and Uncle Sam in his affairs overseas – I seen my fair share of bullet wounds, and done my turn with a field dressing, might be some years but they say it's not as what you know, but… what you remember.'

He left, there were noises behind me, and he came back with a cool drink of water.

'It's just a graze, it's passed over but not through, like the spirit of the Lord.' He was close enough for me to see lines running down under his cheeks bones and the narrowness of his lips in his spare, sun-worn face. I took him to be in his early forties, and I knew I was younger. He pressed a wad of cotton wool to my wound and fastened it with gauze and band-aid.

'This place here's something of a weekend retreat,' he said as he worked, 'something of a bolt hole if you will, for when I have need of it.' He rinsed a cloth and pressed it cold and delicious to my pounding head. 'Normally, its very… isolation is a boon to me, but now I see its limitations.' He took the cloth away. 'No phone, I'm afraid.'

'No phone?'

'No reception - and it so happens that my old S.U.V was makin' a terrible fuss on the way over, so I've got her engine out to see as what I can make of it…'

'So no car…'

He grinned. 'As we find ourselves some forty miles from anything as you might call…' his tongue flickered again, 'civilization, you may have to stop a while.'

'I'm sorry to put you out…' something bobbed up from my memory, then slipped away. There was something I needed to do.

Urgently.

''Taint no trouble, it's only your loved ones of whom I'm thinking, no doubt they're fretting over what has become of you?'

'You don't have a phone?' I asked again, finding I had no desire to call the police and I was relieved neither could he.

'Fraid I don't, as I say - I'm thinking as it would be better for you to close up them pretty eyes and get yourself some sleep.'

I'd already closed my eyes, pretty or otherwise, the sucking, glittering blackness pulling me into the quicksand of the afternoon.

'You just lie back, so as to let your body do what it needs to…'

Okay, but there's something I have to remember…

'…Just close your eyes now… the better to start fixing what ails you so.'

But I have to be somewhere, I have to do something - I have to get to…

'…You always did seem too fine for him.'

Paris?

Jeeper's creepers, where d'you get them eyes?

It's all about playing the game, you know that.

Lisa.

Just who you been playin' all along?

Where'd you get them eyes?

Paris.

I woke suddenly with a memory shattered around me. I jerked up and scanned the room, my heart pounding. I was still alive.

It was quiet. The still, clean calm of the air meant morning, with the clean light filtering through dirty windows. My fingers gingerly explored the wadding the man had applied …when was that? Yesterday? Three weeks ago?

Damn - still no name.

A thought sniggered at the back of my mind. I was covered in a rough, grey blanket and I raised it – still fully dressed, thank God. However pretty he'd thought my eyes, he'd kept his hands to himself. *Or bothered to dress me again.*

'Good morning.'

The laconic voice came from over my shoulder. I flinched round, and pulled the blanket up as if I were naked, grimacing at the pain.

'Sorry, I did not mean to wake you.'

'I was awake already.' I said, trying to clear my dusty throat.

'You slept okay,' he stated, 'almost like the dead.'

'I'm sorry.' I said, trying to stand, 'I should get going.' He was holding a wrench with a rag wrapped round it.

'Going?' He frowned, working the rag over the wrench. 'It's still early.'

'Did I wake you then?'

'Oh hell no, I've always been an early riser. My mama said as how it's the southern climate, makes one rise with the dawn and take a,' he paused, 'something of a siesta to cope with the heat of the day. An army life behoves a man not to be a slug-a-bed.' He stopped moving the rag. 'I been up a good hour already seein' to the engine, it ain't much after seven.'

'Even so.' My head wasn't pounding but I was groggy. 'I've imposed on you long enough, really I should-'

'Now just you hold on,' he took a step toward me, 'what sort of gentleman would I be, sending a lady out in such a state with no breakfast. Hell, I'd not treat my ex-wife like that, and she did plenty more in the way of imposition.'

'Really, I…' the word 'breakfast' had my stomach growling.

'Shower?' He asked, 'the facilities maybe a little basic, but I spied solar panels and there's hot water a plenty. One thing we do have is too much sunshine.' A shower sounded like the nearest thing to heaven this side of the grave.

'Thank you, but I really don't want to be a burden-'

'Darlin',' he purred, 'sure as I'll be the judge of that. Can't say I have much in the way as would suit you, but I can let you have a clean shirt of mine and some pants as you ain't a whole lot shorter than I. Anyway, seems ladies do dress in a most masculine way these days.'

'Thank you.'

'You got no memory still?' He came a little closer, 'no idea what fate befell you…' he ran the cloth over the wrench, caressing it as if he hoped to summon a genie, 'out there down that dirt track?'

'No.' I said.

'Such a queer thing,' he looked as if I was not the genie he'd been expecting. 'Seems as how I'll have to introduce myself and still be at a disadvantage.' He released the cloth and held out a hand grimed with oil. 'Daddy saw fit to name me Rooster - he's a great fan of John Wayne mind you - but most as knows me, calls me Red.' He waited for me to take his hand, and though it was dirty, I figured mine was worse.

'Nice to meet you, Red.'

'And what we gonna call you then, guess you don't have no I.D.?' I hadn't thought of that; dropping his hand I ran mine over my jeans.

Nothing.

'Suppose you must'a mislaid your purse,' his tongue licked his lips, 'along with your memory.'

'Seems so.' I smiled, wishing he would step away. His eyes were very pale green, with something animal about them.

Seems as if you have the advantage of me….

'So,' he turned, 'you'll find the bathroom at the top of the stairs; I've laid out what I can for you.' He walked into the small kitchen and flung the rag into the sink, put down the wrench and turned on the taps. 'This house is a mean place I'm sure,' he looked back at me, 'but consider all it has to offer at your disposal.' He plunged his hands under the flow of water.

I had to lock the door before I could look at the stranger in the bathroom mirror. I saw myself as one does in a dream, as both the observer and observed. Short dark hair, livid purple bruise on my forehead under my bangs, and rather pretty dark eyes for all they were smudged with dirt and make-up. I reached out and touched the hand reaching for mine with long, dirt-rimmed fingernails. Taller than average, not a bad body either, nice and slim if a little heavy in the seat.

Nice junk in the trunk.

The words came to me with a smile, a laugh and a rush of emotion. The smile grinned at me; the smile sent me reeling back against the door.

Nice junk in the trunk, honey chil' - hate to see you leave, love to watch you go.

The smile was black, the smile was warm, it curled its way deep into my spine, snarled and left me cold and shaking.

Paris. I had to get to Paris.

First, I had to take a shower; the movement caused a day old stink of sweat and blood to rise up round me. Maybe the water would clear my head.

Nice junk in the trunk.

I slid out of my disgusting clothes, noting his clean offering on the rail with two utilitarian towels. If this was his idea of a weekend getaway, he must be Spartan in nature. *No four ply double plush luxury for old Red.*

I peeled off my bandage. The water was good and solar hot as promised; I shivered with delight as it engulfed me. The wound looked ugly but not deep as he'd observed. *How did he know it was bullet wound?* It could have been anything. *Maybe I fell, maybe it was a branch ripping my side or…*

The image came to me like a flashlight in the dark - my hand holding a gun.

I screwed up my eyes and pressed my head against the cold, wet tiles. *Don't force it, let it come.*

What you doin' you crazy bitch! The voice, angry now, spiralled down the plughole with the dirty water.

Red knew me.

I knew Red.

He was surprised to see me not because I was a stranger, but…*because I wasn't.*

Had he shot me?

Had I shot some one?

I sat on the closed toilet and wrapped the towels around me, rubbing furiously.

'You always did seem too fine for him.' Red's voice drifted back to me.

For whom, too fine for whom?

The smile was back, black skin and white teeth. Paris, I had to get to Paris.

I struggled into the shirt, which was too big, too white and a little translucent, and heaved on the jeans. I confronted myself in the mirror.

If Red wanted me dead, I would have been. He could have pressed a pillow over my face and dumped my body in the swamp, so if he knew me, if he knew who I was, he had a reason for not telling. If he thought I remembered nothing at all, maybe I'd buy myself time.

It's only an inch from the truth.

I opened the bathroom cabinet and my face swung away. Safety razor, no use, tooth-powder - *'For the gentle cleansing of dentures and bridge work.'* Red had false teeth? *If I were you Red old boy, I'd find a new orthodontist.* There were pills in a prescription bottle. I didn't recognise the brand, but the label said, *'for the relief of angina, take as directed.'*

Maybe Red's older than I'd thought.

I closed the door and said to my reflection, *'you need to eat and drink, 'cause you ain't going nowhere running on empty. Then you get out, whatever it takes.'*

Still smarting from their forgotten journey, my feet carried me back downstairs and I tried to adopt the air of one feeling nothing but gratitude. He looked up from the stove and smiled a crocodilian welcome.

'It ill behoves me to make such an observation to a lady, but you look mighty refreshed and much improved by your toilet.'

I returned the smile as easily as I could and walked toward him. The place seemed smaller than yesterday, the kitchen a tiny offshoot of the main room.

'You'd care for coffee? I fear it's only instant, but we are limited for supplies. I was not...,' he opened a cupboard above the stove then closed it again, '...expecting to entertain.' He located a kettle, a jar of coffee, a large skillet and mugs. 'No milk, I'm sorry to say, but then I like mine black.' He drummed a teaspoon on the lid of the jar.

'That's fine, I take mine black.' I said, and smiled without warmth.

'I dare say as you do.' He licked his lips, and turned away.

I leant against the doorframe and watched him work; trying to glimpse what was concealed in the kitchen drawers.

'I don't claim to be much in the way of a chef,' he said as a halo of blue fire erupted under the kettle at his touch. 'My mother, she was the real cook in our family, when she was minded to send the maid home,' he paused by the icebox. 'You look as if it surprises you to hear as how we had a maid when I was a boy.'

'Oh, no, it doesn't...'

Red smiled. 'I'm not always as you see me here, as I say, this place is something of a refuge for me. A place of...' he took out raw bacon and eggs, '...a place of discovery, one might say.'

He flicked the gas on under the skillet and added bacon, fat moistening the iron surface. My stomach howled and gnawed in protest, hunger made me giddy. *Focus.*

'We learned a thing or two, when we was serving Uncle Sam - how to cook eggs on the bonnet of a vehicle, that sort of amusement.' He turned the bacon and picked up an egg. 'I cooked this for my wife, I was married once you understand, but serving the flag is not kind on the state of marriage.'

'I'm sorry,' I said almost abstractedly, watching as he cracked the egg.

'You still have no memory of how you came by here?' The egg turned from glass to porcelain as it hit the pan.

'No.' He looked a little sharply at me. 'Nothing, I'm real sorry.'

'No need to apologise. Seems as if you're a long way from home, by the timbre of your voice, all with no memory of how to return.' He flipped the bacon, and turned toward me. 'Should I impose on you, then?'

'Sorry?'

He smiled, 'I'm accustomed to calling a lady Ma'am and it don't bother me at all, but if you're of a more modern mind, perhaps I might venture to offer you a name?'

'I guess, seeing as I know yours,' I said, a warning prickling down my spine as he came closer. I had the feeling that I should embrace him, or that I once had. My palms ached with delicious repulsion.

'I had an Aunt once, and you bring her to mind, not that she was anything as well formed as you,' he chuckled, 'but when I knew her, she had no memory, so maybe that's why I light on her... Margarita?'

'Sorry?' He wanted me to own it.

'Her name was Margarita.' His gaze flickered over me, 'like the drink - she was partial to one or two, in her day.' He watched as if trying to tell the time from an unfamiliar clock. 'I like 'em easy,' he said.

'Easy?'

'Yes.' He was inches away, the smell of food making my mouth water. I could see the pulse in his neck and the hard, spare muscle of his chest under the tight grey shirt he wore. 'I've always preferred them easy, my eggs, how d'you take them... Margarita?'

I inhaled the scent of him, made glorious with the smell of breakfast. I met his gaze and released the smile hiding in my mouth. 'I like mine hard.'

'Hard?'

'Real good and firm, that's what I prefer.' He looked down for a moment, something lazy and eager playing over his lips, pulling them into a grin.

'I better go see to the pan,' he turned on his heel and flipped a kitchen cloth over his shoulder in the manner of a short-order cook. 'Go sit at the table,' he instructed as he got out two plates. 'Be ready in a moment.' He smiled his crocodile smile.

He set the food down. I was so hungry I'd eaten half before I looked up and sensed his mood change. I swilled a mouthful of coffee, and said lightly. 'Forgive me; I'm just so hungry.'

'Good to see a lady enjoying her ham and egg,' he said mirthlessly.

'As soon as I, as I get somewhere...' I swallowed more bacon, '...then I'll send you some money.'

'Money?' He frowned.

'You've been so kind, at least let me pay for the gas to go to town.'

'Yes, about that.' He smiled over his coffee. 'Seems as how I'd done a little more to my poor old truck than I'd intended.'

'What do you mean?' I set my fork down.

He smiled, but turned it into a leer as he cleared his teeth. 'She won't be going anywhere for a day or so, still haven't got her going again.' Now I wanted to run. 'Seems as how you'll be stopping a while yet.'

'How far is it?' I said. 'I'll walk.'

He raised an eyebrow and tilted his head a little. 'On those poor little shoes? You've already walked them through to the sole Margarita, thin as prison gruel.'

'Well-'

'Sure you wouldn't rather rest up and get your strength back?' He placed his knife and fork together on his plate and lent forward on his elbows. 'You ever made love in the supple, wet heat of the afternoon, Margarita?'

A cold shiver inched its way down my spine. 'Okay, that's-'

'You ever just let the day lie heavy on you and slip off your cares for a while? Give yourself over to pleasuring the flesh?'

'What the hell are you-'

'Well, you're a sweet piece of ass, and even my ex-wife would confess, that I am a fine and considerate...' he picked up a napkin and dabbed the corner of his mouth. '...lover. Were she still here.'

I scraped my chair back across the floor and he went for me. The table crashed over and the breakfast things exploded onto the floor. I was too slow to stop him snatching my wrist and yanking me toward him.

'You still don't have no mind to remember?' He snarled, 'you cheap little whore!'

I didn't scream, I went limp and tried to drop to the floor, dragging him down to try and break his gip, but he was stronger, faster and went with me. He got me onto the floor, his knee in the small of my back and twisted my hands together. His training at Abu Ghraib was not wasted. I struggled until instinct told me to lie still.

'You done yet?' He panted over me, 'we ready to talk now?'

'Please,' I said, 'let me go.'

'Now why...' he said, his mouth close to my ear, '...would I do a fool thing like that, pretty? You gonna stop with all this pretence now?'

'Pretence!' I sobbed, 'please, I don't know what you want from me!'

'Really?' He laughed, and let me go. The shock of it made me cry out. I twisted myself onto my side to see what he was about. Laughing, he flung his arms, shaking down his hands and turned to a small side table. He took a gun from the drawer and pointed it at me.

'I do hate to resort to such crude tactics, but there it is. I've been waiting to see when you was gonna crack, but I'm starting to wonder, are you telling me the truth, pretty?'

I drew my legs slowly up towards my chest, 'Okay, okay Red.' God I hurt, and I was pretty sure my wound was bleeding again. 'Please – I know we've met before but I don't know when or what happened …I'm guessing you don't want to kill me.'

'You sure of that?' He shrugged exaggeratedly. 'Why? For the colour of your eyes, pretty?'

He threw himself onto the sofa, gun still pointed at me. 'But hell, I guess you're clever enough to figure that out, memory or no memory.' He coughed, and it shook him more than I expected.

My side jabbed with pain as I moved, 'did you shoot me?' I demanded.

'Me?' He looked surprised. 'Whatever crimes are laid at my door, that ain't one of them. Paris shot you.'

Paris. The word impacted harder than he had – and with it something that started to reform reality. Paris - a smile and the scent of warm skin on a hot day; a collection of light and dark and laughter; Paris whom I'd deceived and who had betrayed me.

'You remember him, do you pretty?' Red leaned forward hungrily. 'I'd be surprised if you don't, seein' as he's the one what shot you.' He lowered the gun a little.

Paris. I had no face, I had no detail but the energy of him warmed something blind inside me.

'You've no idea how surprised I was,' he said, relaxing back a little, 'when I see, as it were, the vixen finding the dog, after I thought the trail gone cold.'

'You were following me?'

'I was following the both of you,' he frowned. 'No, my mistake, please forgive me – I was following my Daddy's money…' he slowly raised the gun again. 'On that note pretty, where is it?'

'What?'

'The bag with my Daddy's fifty thousand dollars in it.'

The room was getting hotter, the smell and damp of the swamp sweating from the earth below. Red stood up, jammed the gun into his belt and held his hand out to me.

'I guess you an' he was working your way through the state, just griftin' along.' He jabbed his hand at me again. 'Get up – I needs to educate you on a few facts.'

He yanked me to my feet. I pulled away from him and sat down. I needed to know what he knew, and I needed a way out. I needed to live. I gripped the edge of the sofa and my fingers encountered a small square of duct tape.

'So,' Red thrust his hands into his pockets and rocked back on his heels. 'Whatever reason, you and your fine young buck Paris, fixed on Daddy and me when we were havin' ourselves some father son time.'

I couldn't resist. 'Who's your Daddy?'

'Senator Daddy to you, bitch.' Red had not seen the same films as I. 'A good man, with a son who's been a sorry disappointment to him.'

'You surprise me,' I muttered. The precise placement of the duct tape on the sofa cushion seemed familiar. I was distracted when Red laughed and hit me across the face, hard enough to have me on the floor again.

'I like you better on your knees, whore!' He spat and wiped his mouth.

Sucking air into my lungs, holding in my sob I saw stars, then something glinting stuck to the underside of the sofa, arranged precisely in line with the tape like a compass pointing true north.

Red continued, 'My Daddy's a man of old-fashioned tastes and vices, even he needs to let off a little steam from time to time.' Red picked up the chair he'd knocked over with the table and sat on it.

'It was a fine hustle; you even had me fooled. Daddy has...,' he smiled, '...traditional ideas when it comes to a sweet little thing like you with a big old nigger like Paris.' He relished the filthy word. 'Staking you in a poker game, guess that really appealed to the old man, specially as he thought he couldn't lose, what with you twining yourself about so... invitingly.' He dripped my life's poison in my ear. 'But Daddy wants his money back, and he can't be seen to dirty his hands, pretty, with you and your,' he tilted his head, 'boy.'

He was blocking the main door. The kitchen with its exit was to my left, he saw me risking a glance up, and when he looked to see where, I slid my hand under the sofa.

'So, I been following you two.' He smiled, 'special ops training, courtesy of Uncle Sam. Just took my time - like my wife, you never realised I was watching.'

I glanced at his gun as my hand closed around the handle of the short, neat hunting knife.

'I suppose you and he had something in the nature of a falling out,' Red scratched the back of his neck. 'Like myself and my wife- perhaps Paris caught you sniffing round his best friend also.'

'Please, I don't know where this money is,' I gasped 'I don't remember.'

Red frowned. 'I guess you don't. I asked Paris, but he only said as how you'd taken off with it, after you made him crash.'

'What did you do to him?'

Red shrugged, 'Do pretty? Why, I came across him. The clerk at the motel you stayed in, said as how you were fightin' when you got into the nice, shiny new sports car you had so recently purchased.' He said the word slowly, *purr*-chased. 'Then the nice gentleman at the gas station, said as how a mixed couple were arguing about some place down this long old road. I came across Paris hours later, in a sorry state.'

I remembered red metal. A dry road lined with malformed hangman's trees. Running, I was running.

'Seems as how you and he fought.' Red stood up, the chair between his legs. 'Seems as how you left him bleedin' in the wreck of his new car-'

'No!'

'Seems as how he shot you... you seem less surprised by that notion.'

The memory of pain, hot and white lanced through my side 'Was he... when you left him?'

'Dead?' He rolled the word round his teeth. 'Not when I left him, but I could see as how he were bleeding most profusely. Hot day, long way from anywhere.'

Red car, '*nice junk in the trunk, honey chil'*.

'He made it clear to me that you were gone with my Daddy's money, so I left him to his own devices.'

'You left him to die?'

'I left him on the path you set him, pretty. He made his choice when he hustled Daddy, when you hustled Daddy. Paris was bleedin' pro...fusely, and it were a long, hot day.'

I let a sob catch my throat. 'You let him die for fifty thousand dollars?' I said, drawing the blade toward me.

'Minus expenses.' He stood up, 'I guess two vermin like you couldn't spend that much, even with your nice new car and your cheap motels, you not bein' used to the finer things.'

'And I walked through the door.' The appalling symmetry almost made me smile. I tensed myself tightly round the knife.

'Indeed.' He spread his arms wide, 'the path you set upon brought you right to my door. Like I told you, my SUV needed a good seein' to an' I found this place.'

'This isn't your place...'

'Fraid not,' he looked around, 'though I'm thinking of making an offer, should the owner need a quick sale.' He dragged his fingers through his hair. 'Which he might be, a murder does lower property prices so.'

The familiarity of the cold, hard handle of the knife began to cut away at the patchwork of pain and sucking blackness behind my eyes.

'Your wife?'

He smirked. 'You remind me of her, she spoke like a lady but acted like a two-bit whore.'

'She left you?'

'Not so much left as…. as gone before. We're still married, as far as the law's concerned. I believe one has to wait seven years without contact-'

'What was her name?' I breathed, inching my toes round to grip the floor.

'Seven years and then she'll be declared officially dead.'

'What was her name?' I whispered.

'Why so curious?' He took a step closer. 'This all seems such a bother, for the small change in my Daddy's bag.'

'You killed her, didn't you?' Something began to pulse deep inside me.

'Eventually…' he exhaled to the tip of his fingers with relish. 'She broke her marriage vows, made before God. While I was serving my country, she went sneaking round like a she-cat on heat.'

'Her name.' The humid, brooding sound of the swamp and the stirring of the trees whispered around me.

'Seems as I might as well make it two dead whores,' he said softly, 'at the cost of small change in my Daddies bag.' He pulled his lips into a grin, and rolled his tongue between the teeth it revealed. 'Hell, it will be money well spent, now you's awake to enjoy the experience.'

'Name.' I could hear the anticipation in his breathing as he stood over me.

'Lisa,' he tweaked his hand across his mouth. 'Her name was Lisa, and you're gonna learn just quite how she left this world.' He laughed, 'and I'm gonna enjoy teachin' you.'

I ripped myself round and jammed the knife into his thigh. He howled as he crumpled forward and went to hit me, but the handle of his gun found my hand first. It was still in his belt, I found the trigger and squeezed. His leg shattered, I thrust myself into him as he went down. On top of him, his body writhing and kicking under me, I pressed the gun to his temple.

Vengeance exploded into remembrance.

Paris in the car, furious, shouting *'You've been playin' me, what the hell you mixed up in? You want that psycho to find you? I thought this was just about the money?'*

'You'd never have done it, if you knew I wanted to kill him!'

'You crazy bitch, you think you're gonna shoot me?'

'I will if I have to, turn round and go back to that house-'

'No way, you ain't gonna shoot me, I'm driving. …Jesus Christ!'

He made grab for me, the car jerked away from him and crashed into the side of the road.

The tick-tick of the engine; the second of calm before I tore open the door, grabbed the bag and ran, moving as if the world were molasses.

'Come back with my money – I'll shoot – I'll fuckin' shoot you!'

White pain, then blackness.

I grabbed Reds hair and wrenched his face up to mine. 'Lisa was my sister. You think I'd let anything stop me from getting to you, Red? I remember now, I even got here first.'

The slender thread of letters and emails from Lisa, our only contact since her spectacular falling out with our parents, was severed three years ago. Three days ago, I drove here and planted the knife ready, three months after I'd tracked down Red and set my plan. Paris thought it was all about the money, Paris who had been Lisa's lover. Paris who never knew I was her sister, but knew Red and just what he'd like.

Wracked with coughing, Red's face twisted as he looked at me. 'Seems as though I was right,' his laugh bubbled blood over his thin dry lips. 'You were wasted on him, pretty.'

I took my time over shooting him again, then walked into the kitchen and got myself a glass of water. I slung the gun in the sink, and sauntered back to Red as he sobbed.

'Seems I'm gonna impose on you just a little longer.' I drank, as the inky pool of his blood soaked into the floor, right though to the skin.

After I watched him die, I left for Paris.

4. THE ORPHANED CITY

Kate Robinson

A monster had been born in the city of London.

Bronson had heard the rumours months ago, but had dismissed them as morbid fantasy. It was well known that London had been cleansed almost ten years ago, along with the other major cities in England and Scotland. The genocide had left deep scars on both sides and Bronson could not believe that any monster would return to this city so soon after such an act.

Despite this logic, the rumours had continued and eventually Bronson had felt it necessary to look closer. He sought evidence. It had taken weeks and he had followed the rumours from Kensington to Croydon, finding little. Until, that was, he looked under the streets.

It was a tube station that eventually yielded the first sign. There were tracks in the dust, similar to a man's boot. But with four small scratch marks in front. An untrained eye would have easily mistaken the tracks for a man's footprint. They would have missed the almost inconspicuous extra marks, or dismissed them, but Bronson knew better. He had seen these tracks before. These small marks were caused by claws that had burst through the leather of boots. *And they do not belong to any man.*

Bronson followed the tracks into the darkness of the Piccadilly line. The air was dank beyond the platform and smelt strongly of fuel. His nose burned after a few moments and a pain started in his head. *Must keep going.* The air hummed around him and his footsteps crunched as he trudged through a myriad of insect and rodent life. There was little chance of avoiding them in the darkness. Rats scuttled around his feet, the slower ones letting out shrill squeaks when they were not quick enough to avoid Bronson's feet. The sound of them all around him made his skin crawl.

He could hear the echo of trains. *I hope they are a long way off.* He tried to focus on that hope as he made his way further into the tunnel. He realised he had lost the tracks as he had gotten further away from the light of the station, but it did not worry him. *There's only one way anything the size of a man can go down here.*

The further he went, the darker it got and Bronson argued with himself about using his torch. It would help him see, but it would also mean that any creature down here would be far more likely to see him before he saw it. *With the amount of noise I'm making, anything down here will hear me first anyway.*

The darkness was making a thorough search difficult and his mind kept providing interesting visuals on what would happen to him if he tripped down here. *How long would it take to become buried under the rats?* Bronson stopped and forced himself to take in a few rank breaths. He coughed into his sleeve and wiped his head. *It's getting hotter.* Something crawled over his boot and he shook it off. He had always known that there were rats down the tunnels, but this was a lot more crowded than he had expected. They were everywhere. *I hate rats.* He began wondering how they all lived down here. *What do they eat besides each other and the insects?* Surely there had to be something else. *Perhaps these scavengers have acquired a new source of food.*

Walking was becoming difficult, the heat, blindness and rodent infestation made it heavy going for the hunter. But he was not a coward and slowly he progressed, carefully feeling out where he was walking with each step. Suddenly a sound that seemed to emanate from Hell itself made him freeze in his tracks. His heart raced as he realised he had stepped on what must have been a cat. Bronson let his breath out sharply and cursed to himself. *The wretched creature must have fled or I would have found him by now.* Bronson turned the way he had just come to continue his verbal abuse when he spotted the faintest glint in the gloom just off from the tracks. *Probably just some rubbish that had been dropped on the platform and blown down here.* His gut told him differently.

The glint turned out to be the light from the distant station hitting a watch face. It had once been expensive, but was now cracked, broken and worn by a dead man. The body had been pushed up against the wall and folded tightly into a depression. Bronson cursed as he realised that he must have walked right past it. *Couldn't have been more than two feet away.* Taking a deep breath of burning air, Bronson grabbed a cold arm and pulled. The body came out easily enough with a few tugs and unfolded onto the ground. Bronson turned away, and thanked any God that would listen that the overpowering smell of fuel, heat and filth meant he could not smell the body.

A few moments were all he needed to be able to look back at the body and see that it was not a man. *At least, it's no longer a man.* It was a clue, a trail to follow. His eyes had adjusted to the darkness enough that he could see that this body had been fed from. Most of the clothing was gone and what was left had been shredded so the monster could get to the meat. The teeth marks, shredded flesh and absence of certain organs were well known signs to all hunters. Bronson reached a conclusion. *There's a ghoul in London. A fledgling, barely six years old by the look of the claw marks.*

When he had learned all he could stomach, he put the body back. It took him longer to fold the body back up and push it into the depression. He stopped several times to breathe and more than once considered just leaving the body where it was. *Can't let the Ghoul know that I have found its larder, it would be more careful, can't risk losing track of it.* No point calling the police. *Too many questions, with answers they are unlikely to want to hear. How do you explain that you were in the tunnel hunting monsters?* So Bronson struggled with the body until it was back inside the depression. Then he walked away, scuffing as many of his own tracks as he could find.

Once outside, Bronson took time to suck in great mouthfuls of fresh air. He fumbled with a cigarette, but his hands were shaking too hard for him to manage a light. *Damn ghouls.* Giving up, he began the walk back to his makeshift office, a small and shabby room above a kebab shop. He thought hard as he walked. *No need to hunt the ghoul now, all I have to do is wait.* Ghouls were rarely wasteful and he was confident this one would return to the body. His hands were still trembling by the time he reached the shop. He dropped his keys trying to open the door. *Been a long time since I had to kill a young one.* Looking up, Bronson saw Jimmy, the owner of the kebab shop, waving him inside, as he did most nights.

'You want some dinner?' asked Jimmy, his smile fading when Bronson stepped into the brightly lit shop. 'You look like you need it, or a drink.' Bronson shook his head.

'Naw,' he breathed, pleased that the smell of food did not make him lose what he had eaten this afternoon. 'I'm not sure if I'm ever going to eat again.'

Jimmy winced. 'Another domestic?' he asked, Bronson nodded. It was easier to let Jimmy come to his own conclusions about what he did for a living. Jimmy had assumed he was a police officer at first, but had later amended that opinion to private detective. Bronson found it was safer to let Jimmy think what he liked, it was easier that way too.

'Yeah, bad one,' he managed. 'I'm gonna go lie down.'

'You change your mind about that dinner later, come on down, I'll be here 'til 4.' Jimmy waved at Bronson's back as he went back outside to the small grubby door that would take him upstairs.

Bronson stumbled into his office and flicked on a light. He looked around and sighed. He lived in his office, which was really more of a small flat. *A very small flat.* He ambled into the bathroom and splashed cold water on his face, before stumbling back into the kitchen-bedroom-living room-office. The sofa, which also doubled as his bed, creaked as he fell onto it. He lay there in the dim light and tried to think what to do. *I'll go back to the station. I'll wait and when the Ghoul shows itself I'll act, fast and sudden.* The element of surprise, the plan was simple, effective and had worked dozens of times before. *The ghoul would be lost in its meal.* There was no reason it would not work this time.

*

For three nights Bronson returned to the station and waited. For three nights he had seen no sign of the Ghoul. It was late on the fourth night. *Where are you ghoul?* Looking down at his watch Bronson sighed. The watch had stopped working years before and was now only correct twice a day. He didn't need it and had only kept it for sentimentality. It had been a gift. It didn't matter that the hands no longer moved. He knew only ten minutes had passed since he had entered the station this evening and settled to wait and watch.

Bronson tried to subdue his impatience, but it was a flaw that he often succumbed to. *My failing.* As he sat in the cold station his mind began to wander. Five years ago he had been impatient with Lucy. She had been small, beautiful and unbelievably strong. It was why he had been drawn to her, why he had started to train her. *Why I had loved her.* But she had been too young. He should not have tried to teach her. She still had too much of her childish confidence. *Too naive.*

She had believed she was invincible. She was not invincible and the creatures had been all too willing to prove this point to them both. He could still remember the night she had died. It had replayed itself so often in his nightmares since. He had heard her fear and desperation as she cried out to him, but it was her eventual silence that had been worse. Guilt had eaten at him for a long time. *So sorry.* He had come close to quitting, just putting this life behind him, but it was his duty to protect London and eventually he had picked his shotgun back up. *Revenge.*

Bronson shook himself out of the memory. *Got to stay focused on the hunt.* The station was busy during the day and early evening, but at this time of night there were rarely people around and it was deathly quiet. He had settled against one of the walls, wrapped himself in blankets and tried to look inoffensive. The floor was cold, but that helped keep him awake and alert. He had carefully chosen this position on the first night. It was close to the entrance to the tunnel, but not too close. He was confident that this was where he would eventually find his quarry.

The tunnels were a web beneath London but he did not worry that the ghoul would hide in them for long. Ghouls were not subterranean. *They are fliers, not diggers.* He was convinced his prey would enter from the street, not the tunnels, and if spooked his prey would be far more likely to flee to the sky than the ground.

A sudden movement caught his eye and he tried not to flinch. He bowed his head low and kept watch out of the corner of his eye. His target emerged, not from the street as he had expected, but from the tunnel. It was small, clearly an adolescent, and walked hunched. It held itself like an elderly man bent in the middle. But it moved smoothly like a young man, nimble and fast. Bronson growled before he could help himself. *Disgusting creature. In my city.* Nothing moved quite like a ghoul, apparently decrepit, but deceptively agile. Bronson watched and waited for the fledgling ghoul to move up the stairs and out onto the street. He waited a few moments before following behind.

His shotgun rested comfortably between his shoulder blades, it had been made to fit there and did so perfectly. It had been modified to deal with creatures like this. The round it fired would do enough damage to cripple, or possibly kill, the fledgling ghoul if his aim was good. He reached behind his back and ran his fingers over the barrel. Touching its cold steel at the start of a hunt had become a ritual, like flicking a switch. Bronson, felt himself become sharply focused. He grinned fiercely as he stalked the ghoul. *Time to die.*

The creature stank. Bronson could smell it as he emerged onto the street. The ghoul was keeping to the shadows ahead of him, moving with surprising speed in the direction of the river. Bronson held back and muttered a curse under his breath. The closer he got to the river, the more crowded it would become. *Can't fight a ghoul in a crowded place. Can't risk people discovering that there really are monsters in the dark.* Bronson knew it would result in panic. *And people do unbelievably stupid things when panicked.* Fortunately, the ghoul understood that it could not risk detection any more than Bronson could and it turned east before coming too near to the river. Bronson began to slowly close the distance between them.

As he got closer he started to make deliberate sounds. He hoped to frighten the creature into panicking. Eventually he knocked a can and the ghoul turned. Its eyes widened when it saw him. Its animal intelligence recognising danger, even though it had never met a hunter before, the ghoul knew that it had become the hunted. The creature screeched loudly and ran. Bronson laughed, pulled his shotgun from its holster and gave chase. The ghoul was fast, but it was young and had not yet learned all that it was capable of. Bronson was able to keep pace with it as it turned corner after corner, trying to lose him in the small streets and alley ways. He was still confident. *Just like old times.* The ghoul was panicking and would make a fatal error all too soon. *Then it's mine.* The ghoul disappeared around another corner and Bronson followed, running flat out.

He banked hard as he found himself running right into the creature's back. It had run into an alleyway and frozen in panic. It was staring frantically at its surroundings, looking for a way out. But there was nowhere else for it to run. *They always make a mistake.* Bronson jumped back far enough that the ghoul could not reach him. The creature could shred a man in seconds and even a fledgling had claws like knives. The ghoul turned and looked at him. Bronson met its gaze.

It was small, no bigger than a pre-teen boy. Its face was almost human, save from a few tell tale signs. The eyes were too big and the mouth too wide. This one had not got the hang of its camouflage yet. It snarled, showing teeth, sharp like razorblades, long and serrated. Bronson growled right back. The young ghoul took a step back and glanced around, still searching for a place to run.

'Ain't nowhere left for you to run, beast,' Bronson sneered. 'You shouldn't have come here. Didn't your foul mother warn you London ain't safe for your kind no more?'

'Mumma,' the ghoul screamed into the night. Bronson frowned. *Never heard a ghoul call for its mother before.* It was disconcerting. In his bewilderment he didn't notice the young ghoul tense its body.

'Mumma,' it called again. By the time the word was out of its mouth it had leapt upwards, faster than any human eye could follow. Its claws dug deep into brick work and it clambered ungracefully up the wall, slipping every few feet, but regaining its footing each time. The brickwork was old and it crumbled. It was not strong enough to hold the creature's weight.

'That won't save you.' Bronson grinned, 'I don't need you to be close to kill you.' He lifted his shotgun.

He was taking aim when it finally reached his brain that he was in trouble. He had been so focused on the fledgling that he had failed to notice a new, stronger smell had entered the alley. He also hadn't noticed how still the streets around them seemed to be. A chill trickled over Bronson's shoulders as he finally noticed how unusual and how wrong this was. *Nowhere in London is this quiet, unless it had been purposefully made quiet.* He looked away from the fledgling on the wall and cursed himself. He had been foolish to follow so unquestioningly, he was out of practice and had let his impatience rule him. He hoped it would not cost him too dearly.

The adult ghoul slid soundlessly out of the shadows and into the alley. *The mother.* She moved silently like fog and from her posture Bronson knew she too was hunting. *No doubt she has been from the moment the fledgling walked past me at the station, perhaps even before that. A trap.* It had been carefully executed. This ghoul was clever. Bronson watched as she approached. Female adult ghouls were smaller than the males, weaker and unable to fly. But they were fiercer by far. Ghouls bred rarely and the young often died. But it was never because a mother was not willing to shred anything that dared to interfere with her child. A mother ghoul with a child was something rare and deadly. He had taken down only one before. *That hunt had cost seven men.* It was suicide to take on an adult female alone.

Bronson took a deep breath. *If I'm going to die tonight, I'm going down fighting.* The mother ghoul stopped in front of him and smiled. Recognition was triggered in his mind. In the light he knew her and was no longer surprised at the trap.

'I have heard of you, Myra,' he said slowly. The adult ghoul seemed surprised at this, although whether it was because of the words, or the fact Bronson found voice to speak at all, he didn't know.

'Some have,' she replied. 'More know my brother.' Bronson nodded. He knew of Tobias, all hunters did. It had been one of the great hunts. It was rumoured that they captured Tobias alive so that they could torture him into revealing the secret ways of the ghouls.

'I was hunting,' Bronson spared a glance to the fledgling ghoul on the wall.

'As are we.'

'I thought you might be, but I hoped against it.' Bronson lifted his shotgun and took aim at the mother ghoul.

'I suppose I cannot fault you for that.' With those words Myra lunged. But not at Bronson, as he had expected. Instead she threw herself to the side to avoid the bullet Bronson had fired. What killed Bronson were the claws in the back of his neck. They slid in roughly, tearing the skin instead of slicing it. They came together and pulled, breaking the spinal column and removing a large fleshy pulp along with bone. Bronson fell, paralysed and dying.

'Well done.' Myra picked herself up from the ground. 'But you are still not using the smooth side.' She took her son's hand and showed him his claws. Gently she ran a finger over the serrated side and then the smooth side. 'Remember, smooth going in and rough coming out.'

'Yes mumma,' the fledgling nodded, licking the blood from his claws. 'Are we safe now? The hunter is dead.' Myra sighed and looked at what was left of Bronson.

'We are safer. But we are not safe. Not yet.' She looked again at Bronson. 'Go and eat child. His memories will teach you much about the dangers of the hunters and, if we are lucky, you might just find out where you can meet your Uncle Tobias.'

5. THE HASSAM LEGACY

A G Lyttle

Ryan Horsham couldn't decide whether he was the luckiest man alive or the most wretched. He was facing bankruptcy at the age of twenty-five. It was little consolation that it resulted from the failure of Jean-Claude's brilliantly-conceived dot com company that he had helped finance with pretty much all his worldly wealth, only to have it brought to its knees through massively unfair tactics from two of the internet giants.

And yet here he was, sitting on a Paris bench in the Place Denfert-Rochereau, sunlight filtering through the leaves of the horse-chestnut trees and dappling the ground where sparrows were hopping about looking for crumbs – and, beside him, the most beautiful girl he had ever seen.

*

When Lara had turned up at his bed-sit in Paddington the day before yesterday, Ryan had just stood there, transfixed.

'Well, aren't ya going to go ahead and invite a gal in, cousin?'

Ryan had recovered himself sufficiently to usher in the stunning 'gal' with her long waves of chestnut hair and perfect oval face that smiled up at him as she passed into his room. She didn't seem to mind the clutter. She shoved some old newspapers aside and flopped down on the sofa. Her mini-dress revealed much more than it concealed.

'I'm Lara Moffatt. From Boston. And you're Ryan Horsham.'

Ryan wasn't sure if she'd finished with a question or a statement, but in his bemused condition he was grateful enough for the confirmation.

'Got me in one,' he managed to reply. 'Eh, did you just call me cousin as you came in? We had relatives emigrated to Boston, way back.

'I know! And you're my third cousin, six times removed – or something silly like that. I've just finished Art School. French Impressionism. I'm 'doing' Europe. My mother's great-uncle was Frederick Childe Hassam.' She accented the first syllable of the surname. 'Heard of him?'

'Well, I know the branch that emigrated changed their name from Horsham to Hassam. I vaguely remember my gran talking about an artist in the family called Childe. So he's some sort of great-great uncle of mine? Six times removed.'

Lara laughed. 'I guess he is, too. He was quite famous. Probably the most famous American Impressionist.'

She made it sound quite matter-of-fact and Ryan caught himself wondering if he was as good as Rory Bremner. Perhaps fortunately, he had no time to voice his thoughts before this beautiful creature, who was so unexpectedly languishing on the sofa of his bachelor pad, continued.

'When he studied in France, he knew all the greats – Lefebvre, Monet, Degas and Caillebotte – '

'Did he, now? I never realised we were so well connected.'

As Lara went on, filling in some background and explaining how she had found his address through a series of intermediary relatives, each of varying degrees of removal, Ryan thought he noticed an excitement creeping into her tone.

'And the thing is, Coz – why I really needed to find you first – I'm on a sort of treasure hunt! I don't have any French cousins, but you're only just down the street, so you'll do fine.'

'Down the street?'

'From Paris. It's only a couple of hundred miles from London. We could practically walk it.'

'It's in a foreign country! It's across the Channel. They don't speak English – or American.'

'Oh, don't be a fuss-pot! I can't do this alone. Will you help me?'

Ryan thought he had never seen such large, brown eyes as Lara's as they gazed, appealingly, into his own. 'Of course,' he couldn't help but reply, 'if you think I can.' And Lara had flung her arms round his neck and kissed him.

*

He had gotten over the embarrassment of finding he did not have enough credit left on his card to pay for his own Eurostar ticket, never mind Lara's, but she had insisted on covering all the expenses anyway. She also insisted that, if they did find the 'treasure', which apparently was by no means certain, he should have half of it.

Lara had explained it all during their Chunnel journey and Ryan found himself with mixed feelings. It could just be the miracle he needed to clear all his debts and give him a fresh start. But considering the chances of it actually succeeding, he was just grateful his return ticket was already paid for.

*

They sat in the little park that was actually the centre of one of the largest roundabouts Lara had ever seen, where Boulevard Raspail met seven other thoroughfares in the French capital. She was thinking how lucky she was that 'cousin' Ryan had turned out to be such a cute guy. It didn't bother her that he didn't seem to have much money. He was athletic and funny and had an adorable English accent. And he had a French friend, too, who was going to help them — they'd been students together, apparently, and then ran some sort of joint business venture that hadn't worked out. They'd agreed to meet Jean-Claude here in the park because the treasure, if it still existed, should be nearby.

It was quite amazing, really. Her mother had died last December and they'd only just finished sorting out her things after Lara's graduation in the summer. The diary had almost been thrown in the trash with other old notebooks. It was Lara who had spotted that it wasn't in her mother's hand. It turned out to have been written by her Great-Uncle Childe in 1897. She had read two particular entries so often now that she knew them by heart.

April 3
Crazy party last night in Catacombs. Couple of Frenchies bribed to let us in at midnight. Cream of Parisian intelligentsia, painters, musicians, men of distinction — even let in a few of us refugees from Uncle Sam. The absinthe was flowing freely. Was asked to bring along some of my sketches to swap; then left the dratted things behind in the rush to get out when we were almost discovered! Great caper.

April 10
The darnedest thing. The guys who let us into the catacombs have been fired. Security real tight now. Can't see I'm ever going to get back my sketches. Nobody else likely to either due to that stupid game of hide and go seek we played. Seemed hilarious, though, at two o'clock in the morning last week.

'Let's look at the map again. Jean-Claude should be here any minute.'

Lara produced a folded sheet from her bum-bag and laughed, 'I was just thinking about it, Ryan.'

'Ah, great minds… You're sure this is an exact copy?'

'Of course I'm sure. I made it bigger, but this is what was in the diary. I suppose he drew it so he would remember where his sketches were hidden, if he ever got a chance to retrieve them.'

'But how do you know he didn't?'

'Well– '

'Or that somebody else hasn't. It *was* over a hundred years ago, for goodness sake!'

'We've been over this, Ryan. We won't *know* until we look – if we can get to it. But that's the thing. Nobody *can* get to it – normally. And they'd have no reason to try. No-one but us know they're there!'

Ryan was hoping against hope that they were. He was about to be evicted from his bed-sit. His credit card bill wasn't his only debt. He had nothing left. Nothing. Except the beautiful Lara. He glanced at her and then ridiculed himself. What chance did he have with her with absolutely nothing to offer?

'Ryan! Mon ami. Ça va?'

Ryan stood and embraced Jean-Claude as he strode up. 'Ça va. Ici Lara.'

*

They were in the Catacombs, standing by the Barrel in the Crypt of the Passion, as Jean-Claude's guide book called it. He translated the description for them.

'This Barrel-shaped display of skulls and tibias was built to hide a support pillar. A macabre party was held here on 2 April 1897, from midnight to two in the morning. Intellectuals, artists and distinguished members of the bourgeoisie took part in a secret concert organised by two Catacomb workers, who were dismissed as soon as word of the event got out.'

'So it really happened. Good old Great Uncle Childe stood on this very spot over a hundred years ago at midnight – and left us his legacy.'

'Maybe, Lara. Maybe.' Ryan didn't want to get his hopes up, but now he was actually here, in the very place, it was beginning to seem just possible.

From the entrance near the park, they had descended the endless stairs that took them to twice the depth of the Metro. They emerged into long tunnels that had been quarried out in the 17th century, according to Jean-Claude, who had actually worked in them as a guide one summer vacation. That was why, when they had phoned him from London to ask if he knew whether the tunnels were open to the public, he had offered to come with them for the fun of it. He wouldn't hear of taking any share of their 'treasure'. He said he owed Ryan.

He led them along passageways in subdued lighting, ignoring occasional branches that were roped off to the public, until they reached an archway that lead to what was called the ossuary. He translated the words carved on the lintel.

'Halt, for this is the empire of death.'

As they passed through, Lara gasped and involuntarily grabbed Ryan's hand. She held on tightly.

'Creepy! So many bones.' Ryan gazed around. 'Every wall is lined with stacks of them.'

'Look closer, mon ami.'

Ryan approached one wall. 'They're not lining the wall, are they? They have been built to form another inner wall, themselves. Like a dry-stone-wall of bones!'

'Oui. Layers upon layers of tibia and fibula, laid flat – and then every so often a layer of sculls. So nice, n'est ce pas?'

Lara shuddered. 'It's the skulls staring out at me that give me the heebie-jeebies. Don't let go of my hand, Ryan.'

Ryan had no intention of letting go. He was really beginning to enjoy this, but he was equally amazed at what he was seeing. 'There must be thousands, tens of thousands of skulls here.'

Jean-Claude said, 'Try millions. Here are the remains of six million people. They were dumped any old way at first, but later they built these neat , if somewhat macabre, inner walls and behind them – between them and the tunnel walls – they just dumped all the millions of other bones, like so much builder's rubble.'

They had continued walking as they talked and had arrived at the Crypt of Passion. Lara was looking at her map.

'From the Barrel – that's there,' she pointed, 'it's ten paces… this way. To that wall over there by the roped-off passage.'

The others looked to where she was indicating, a wall of bones about seven feet high. They controlled their urge to rush over as other visitors were around. According to the map, Childe Hassam had left his sketches among the rubble behind this wall. But how to get at them without being seen – not just by the public, but more importantly, by the strategically positioned guards?

They had a plan of sorts. Ryan and Lara could only hope that it would work as they stood nervously by the wall at the point marked on the map. Jean-Claude walked back beyond the Barrel and took out his pocket camera, looking just like a typical tourist. The few people in their vicinity glanced in his direction as his flash went off.

Some distance away a stern voice called out, 'Pas photographie!'

Jean-Claude's camera flashed again.

'Non, M'sieur! Pas photographie!'

The guard was striding rapidly towards the offending 'tourist'. All eyes were turned in his direction as a heated altercation ensued. Lara clasped her hands together and Ryan used them as a stirrup to help him scale the grisly wall. In a moment he was over the top and lying flat on the jumbled pile of bones and broken skulls behind. He shuddered, but he was safely out of sight. He took out his torch and started searching.

Lara joined the small group watching the guard remonstrating with Jean-Claude. As soon as he saw her, he immediately calmed down and became all apologetic. The incident was soon over and forgotten by the other visitors, but the guard and his two colleagues at the other end of the passage were keeping their eyes on Jean-Claude.

'Have you found anything?' Lara whispered, back at the marked wall.

Ryan's voice came back, subdued and disappointed, 'There are no sketches. Nothing.'

Lara's heart fell. 'Are you sure? They'd be rolled up, almost certainly.'

Ryan cursed under his breath. Of course they'd be rolled up! He'd been stupidly looking for sheets of paper lying around, maybe in a paste-board folder. He looked again at all the dusty, grey bones. One had a slightly darker hue. He touched it and recoiled in horror. It felt leathery, as though the skin was still attached. He forced himself to look again. Tentatively, he pulled it from its crevice and blew the grey dust from the surface. He was holding a leather cylinder capped at both ends.

'I've found the treasure!' he shouted out without thinking. The nearer guard glanced up, sharply, and started towards where Lara and Jean-Claude were standing.

'Vite! Come down,' Jean-Claude shouted.

Ryan scrambled over the wall and dropped to the floor. The guard shouted to them to stay right where they were. Instinctively, they headed the opposite way only to be confronted by the other guards rapidly closing from that direction. They were trapped.

'A moi! This way.'

Jean Claude dived into the roped-off tunnel and held up the rope for Lara to duck under.

The first guard made a grab for him as he followed her, but Ryan was just behind and straight-armed the guy out of the way before executing a perfect scissor-kick over the rope to race after the others.

He found himself in a much narrower tunnel that was rough underfoot and rapidly becoming very dark. He flicked on his torch as he ran.

'Come on, Ryan, hurry! Shine the torch ahead.'

'I'm coming, Lara.' He copied the sotto voce urgency she had used and heard her question Jean-Claude.

'Do we know where this leads? There must be miles of tunnels down here. We could easily get lost.'

'Losing ourselves, I think, is preferable to being handed over to the Gendarmes, no?'

'Gee, I can't… say I would prefer…' Lara sounded as though she was getting short of breath trying to keep ahead of their pursuers, 'either of those… options much.'

They arrived at a four cross-ways and their French friend swerved into the right-hand opening. 'Never fear,' he said. 'One of the 'private' entrances to the catacombs is situated in this tunnel. Keep running, but quietly. The guides will not know which path we take.'

They looked back as they entered the side passage. They could hear them some way behind but could see nothing.

'There's no light,' Ryan said. 'They mustn't have had time to get flashlights. That'll slow them. It would be easy to trip on this floor.'

'And easy to miss the opening to the stairs. Ryan, let me have your torch.'

Jean-Claude kept swinging the beam from the floor to the side wall and back to the floor.

They needed to see where they were going, but he also needed to find the way out. In whispers, he told the others how he'd only seen it once. He said there had been quite a number of entrances to the maze of tunnels at one time but most of them were now sealed up. A few weren't, like this one that led up to the cellar of a house in Rue Dareau where Pierre Devereux, one of his fellow vacation guides lived. He had shown it to Jean-Claude.

'There!' Jean-Claude lit up a small alcove to their right.

As they stopped to look they all heard the sound behind them. At least one of the guards had started making his way along their passage and there was a flickering glow.

'Hurry! They're using a lighter to see where they're going'

'But - ,' Lara hesitated, 'there is no door, no steps.'

'Merde! It is not the right alcove. Come, it must be further.'

The sounds of pursuit were getting closer as they hurried forward again.

'Is that - ? No. Keep going.'

They passed two more wall indents before Jean-Claude stopped again. 'This is it! Those arched stones above the alcove - I remember them. The stairs are set in on the left.'

Lara went first; up a short flight of stone steps behind the tunnel wall and found herself on a small platform from where an ancient cast-iron spiral staircase ascended. Ryan joined her, with Jean-Claude close on his heels. The place smelled musty.

'With any luck the guides will miss the alcove in the dark. Let's go!'

'Onwards and upwards,' said Ryan

Lifting your own bodyweight vertically through 65 feet takes a lot of effort. When barely halfway Lara stopped to draw breath and Ryan for one was glad to have to stop behind her.

'Ecoutez!'

They all strained their ears in the darkness.

'What did you hear, Jean-Claude?' asked Ryan.

'Steps - below us, on the stairs.'

They continued to listen as they recovered their breath, but heard nothing more.

'False alarm,' said Ryan.

'OK. Allez.'

A little refreshed, Lara started to climb once more with the others hard on her heels. Despite the rest, when they finally reached the top they were exhausted. They were on another stone platform like the one at the bottom. Opposite them was a large oak door set in a wall made of ancient bricks. Jean-Claude was already shoving against it when, over the noise of their heavy breathing, they heard the distinctive sound of footsteps on the metal treads.

'There *is* someone following us. Hurry, Jean-Claude.'

'Won't it be locked from the other side?'

'It would be, Lara, if it hadn't rusted solid decades ago – fortunately for us, in the open position.'

'Arrêtez! Halt! Go no further.' A head appeared at the top of the spiral stairs.

The heavy door scraped on the floor as it pushed slowly inwards. Lara squeezed through the gap. The Catacombs guard climbed out of the staircase and made to grab hold of Ryan, but in his exhausted state he missed and Ryan made it through the door straight behind Jean-Claude. Together they heaved it shut just as they felt the guard fling himself against it to try to keep it open.

They were in a wine cellar and as well as full racks around the walls there were wooden crates with more bottles of wine in the middle. Jean-Claude kept his foot against the door while Ryan and Lara shifted the crates and stacked them up against the stout oak.

'There's no way that's going to open' Ryan said, as he placed the last crate and then collapsed to the floor alongside Lara and Jean-Claude to recover from his exertions.

Some wooden stairs led up to another door out of the cellar. As they sat on the floor breathing hard, the sound of a key turning in a lock caused them to turn as one and stare at the door. It swung open. Silhouetted in the doorway was an elderly man. He held a musket in his hands and it was pointing straight at Ryan.

*

The accordion music was piped, but the sound of the claxon on the bateau-mouche passing along the Seine was real, as was the Beaujolais Lara and Ryan were sipping at the pavement café. And the sketches spread out on the table before them were real, too.

'We were so lucky that Jean-Claude came with us,' said Lara.

'And knew where that roped-off side passage led.'

'And that old Monsieur Devereux recognised Jean-Claude.'

'Well, quite. And that he believed him when he said he was just showing us the 'secret' entrance.' Ryan paused before going on. 'I think it's as well for the old guy that he did believe us. I'm sure if he'd fired that old gun it would have blown up in his face.'

'I think we've been very lucky, coz. But we did it! You did it. You've found my treasure.'

Ryan grinned, and after a pause he asked, 'Is it... do you... think they're worth a lot?'

There were half a dozen sketches in pastels, mostly of Paris bridges with a couple of flowery ones, lilies and laburnums – all with Childe Hassam's initials in one corner.

'Well, they're not going to make us rich, if that's what you mean,' Lara laughed, 'but they should fetch about $500 each, maybe a bit more.'

Ryan's heart sank. $500? That would make his share $1500, barely £1000. That wouldn't even pay off his credit card.

Lara had pick up one of the paintings and seemed to be studying the initials.

'Anything wrong?' Ryan didn't really care. $500 more or less would make little difference.

'It's the H. It seems different to the others. The cross bar – it's not straight. It's sort of V-shaped.' She was speaking almost to herself. 'It is! It's not an H, it's an M. I thought I recognised the flowers.'

'So what are you saying?'

'This painting. Childe Hassam must have swapped one of his for it. It's signed CM, not CH.'

'And does that make a difference?'

'The water lilies. CM – Claude Monet! Yes, just a bit. It's probably worth about a hundred thousand dollars! Would half of that put you back on your feet, Ryan?'

Ryan grasped Lara's hand, almost speechless. 'Would it?' he laughed.

'Enough to come with me on my tour round Europe?' Those big, appealing brown eyes gazed into his once more.

'Oh yes,' he said, 'enough for that.'

Biographical footnote: The famous American Impressionist painter, Frederick Childe Hassam (the family name was changed from that of their ancestors, the Horshams of Sussex), spent much of 1897 in Paris, as evidenced by half-a-dozen or more of his paintings of Parisian scenes, of that date. He was an associate of a number of prominent French artists, including Monet. Guests at the macabre midnight party in the Catacombs are known to have included 'some visiting Americans'.

6. KNOWING JACK

Angela Kelman

Rebecca thought it strange for the door to be ajar when she returned to the flat. Jack raised his finger to his lips when she entered. His tired face tried to smile - but only tried. Something was wrong. His eyes shifted to the right and back again before he lowered his hand. She suddenly realised what he was doing. *There is someone there. He's giving me a head start.*

Her legs had barely taken her to the foot of the stairs when she heard a gunshot. Her heart began to swim, she needed air. It had all happened too soon. Jack was gone, and now they would be searching for her. It was time to become that grain of sand on the beach.

The life she had planned was over.

*

'Peter, Peter,' Rebecca shouted.

She had been looking everywhere. Peter had never actually learned to take the stick back. Her fault of course. *Never trained him properly.*

'Peter? Have you lost someone?' The voice came from behind with the breeze, startling her slightly.

She looked at the stranger and then back across the park. 'No, no... Peter is my dog. I know, I should've gone for something more dog-like, maybe Rover, or Max, but I was 6 and wanted Peter.' She giggled and called out again, louder this time.

'Ah, Peter-the-dog. Catchy. Do you want some help looking for him, Miss?'

Rebecca turned to face the stranger. His face was handsome, in a scruffy kind of way. He looked like the numerous other people she ignored on her walks with the dog. He was smartly dressed though, in a suit, his tie loose around his neck, the top button of his shirt un-done. *Hard day at the office, perhaps.*

'Sure, why not. Black lab, well he's more grey now than black. Red collar.'

He gave her a 'waiting for instruction' look, but she quickly turned again to continue her search.

'You go that way then and I'll go this way' he said.

It didn't take long for him to find Peter; they appeared from behind some shrubs by the

fence. Rebecca was delighted, of course.

'Thank you so much,' she said.

The stranger let go of Peter's collar, allowing her to take it. He looked pleased with himself. She smiled back at his broad grin. There was something welcoming about his smile. *Something familiar.*

He put his hand out. 'Jack.'

She shook it, smiling even more. 'Rebecca.'

She saw him at the park almost every day after that. They would stop and talk, their conversations and walks growing longer each time. He even started to take biscuits for the dog. Jack was always dressed in his office clothes, with a briefcase on occasions. He was much more mature than her seventeen years, greying around his temples. His life had given him deep lines around his eyes, it seemed. Rebecca found herself starting to like him and she always looked forward to their meetings. Sometimes he would be hiding and try to jump out on her when she passed, although often holding a freshly picked flower for a quick apology.

Jack was polite and complimentary, but he was always the one to end their conversations, sometimes abruptly, as he found he had to rush off somewhere mid-laughter. Rebecca found these times frustrating. Then there were times when she didn't see him at all; she hated those times.

The weeks rolled by and she started to become jealous of that part of his life, the one that always called him away just as they were becoming close. He had never mentioned a wife or girlfriend. This had made her more conscious about her choice of clothing and make-up – something she hadn't bothered with before. She liked it when he noticed. Once he even took a lock of her hair in his fingers, in acknowledgement, after she'd had it cut. Her heart had raced when his hand accidentally brushed against her cheek one time.

She wondered if he felt anything towards her - she was a lot younger than him after all. She hoped she was his type, he had mentioned many things he liked about her. She had never had so much attention before and she was fast becoming addicted.

The familiarity she had felt when they first met had made her feel safe. She realised now that she not only wanted to be around him, she needed to be around him.

*

The season had changed; the park was sparkling with a frost that crunched under foot. Rebecca had started walking alone. Peter was getting too old to accompany her for the long strolls, but she wasn't going to give up her meetings with Jack. She imagined what it would be like to run away with him. She was attracted to his maturity and wanted to become a part of his life from outside the park. She wanted him.

He was different that day. He sat on one of the benches that bordered the footpath, his usual suit abandoned in favour of jeans and jumper. There was something about the way he stared across the open grass that seemed odd to her. *For once, he's not in a hurry.*

'Hi there.' She sat next to him.

He slowly swivelled round to face her.

'No Peter today?' he asked.

'Nah, he's old and can't keep up.' She paused and watched his stare return to the park. 'Are you alright? Day off today?'

He glanced back at her, his brow furrowed.

'No suit,' she hinted.

'Ah, well I don't need that anymore.' He forced a smile. 'Happens to the best of us, and now, it seems, I need to move away.'

Rebecca felt sick, like she had been punched from the inside. There had been no warning. *He hadn't mentioned anything about his job being on the line.* She had gotten so used to him and, in a way, he was the only stable thing in her life.

'Are you moving far, Jack?'

'Yeah, quite far.'

There was a long pause. Rebecca found herself unable to speak; she just couldn't find the words.

He continued, 'You wish you could move, right? You've spoken about it a lot. You could come with me if you'd like?'

It was a thought that had already been running through her head. *Running away, for real. I wonder if all this time he's been thinking it too.*

He took her hand. 'You want out don't you? You told me, remember, you want to get away from your foster parents? Well you're 18 now. Time to fly the nest wouldn't you say?'

Talk of leaving had been a part of many of their conversations over the past couple of months. But that's all it had ever been, just talk. Hindsight. *I never knew he felt so strongly about me.*

In her silence, he continued, 'You could get a job, you would be fine. It's what you've always wanted: to stand on your own two feet.' He dropped her hand to touch her leg. 'Listen, I will be here this time tomorrow if you want to come. I want you to.' Squeezing her knee, he pushed himself up to stand. 'Rebecca?'

'Ok, tomorrow, maybe.' She managed a smile, though her heart was racing. *So much to think about.*

She sat alone on the bench and watched him leave. *Foster parents won't be happy about this, especially since the dreams have started again. Maybe I won't tell them everything.* They had wrapped her up tight her whole life. *Too tightly.* Rebecca was 6 when she witnessed her parents being murdered. She had dreamed about it almost every night for a long time. She couldn't be left alone. That's why she had been given a dog. *Peter.* She had named him after her dad and while she was being re-homed he became her best friend. But Peter didn't have long left and now Jack had become her protector. *Can't lose them both.* Her decision had been made.

Jack laughed when she turned up the next day with Peter.
'What? I'm not going anywhere without him,' she said, her arms folded in mock defiance.
He bent down to rub his face. 'Good, I like him.' He scanned the area around her feet. 'Are we going to pick up your stuff?'
'No this is it.' She had a rucksack on her back that she showed with a turn.
'Either you always travel light, or, you didn't tell your parents what you were doing?'
'Well both actually. But I left a note. I couldn't be bothered with the judging and the questions and the arguments.'
He shrugged. 'You're the adult. The car is this way.'

There was talk of phoning her foster parents during the car journey. They had her number, but the note had said not to bother calling if they were going to be disapproving – she'd chosen her path. *I'll wait for them to call first.*
It was a few hours in the car to get to Jack's flat. Except it wasn't really Jacks. He had been allowed to stay there until he got a job and found his own place. It was small, but had everything they would need, including just one bedroom that Rebecca shared with Peter.

*

The days started to go by in a blur. There was nothing biting in the job front. They knew their money wouldn't last forever but they were comfortable enough for the meantime. Rebecca felt less comfortable with Jack though, she had too much time to think. *What role am I playing? What does he want me for?* There had been a few times when she thought she knew what he wanted and had tried to kiss him, sometimes it lingered a while but he would always eventually push her away. *Tells me I'm just a kid, that I don't really want this.* But Rebecca did and she didn't know why he didn't.

*

They had been in the flat for a month when Peter passed away. Jack had gone with her to the vet, supported her. Rebecca had used his phone to let her foster parents know, her own having gone missing. *Must've fallen out of my pocket - everything's going missing these days.* Together they had buried the ashes in the small garden to the back of the flat. But Peter's death became the trigger for her nightmares to return. Jack would come to her in the night when he heard her scream, hold her, but when she came round and explained what she saw he would push her away again - leave her for the couch.

'What do you want from me?' she shouted one night when he had refused her again. 'Am I that awful that you push me away every night? Why am I here, Jack? Why did you ask me to come with you?'

'You need to go back to sleep, Rebecca. We can talk in the morning.'

'No, I'm sick of talking to you. I want you.'

'No you don't, I'm twice you age.'

She had heard it before.

'I don't care. I really don't - you confuse me.' She crawled across the bed to grab his arm and he slowly turned to face her. 'I don't care, Jack. If that's it, I don't care. I know you, I know what I want.'

He laughed, but didn't turn away. Rebecca stared into his eyes. *There's something different about him.* She could feel him giving in. He brushed her hair away from her cheek and moved his hand around the back of her neck, pulling her face close to his.

'You really think you know me don't you?'

There was an instant when all she felt was his breath, and then he let his lips move across hers, at first so softly. She pulled at his top to guide him on to her. She felt the heat of his hand smooth over her hip, creep over her ribs; his lips didn't leave hers. She had wanted this for so long.

He inched his face away from hers and kissed the tip of her nose. 'Listen. Who do you see in your dreams?'

Her eyes searched his, she was confused. 'I've told you.'

She had told him often about her dreams. The men she saw in them, how they had fought and killed her parents in cold blood. *Now's not the time for this.*

He ran his lips over her jaw. 'Do you remember how you escaped, Rebecca?'

'I can't...I was found. You know this.'

'I know. You told me.' He pulled further away from her, raised himself in to a straddle position - his hands gliding up her arms to pin her wrists on the bed, holding her stare.

Rebecca was restrained, she held still waiting for him to let her up but he didn't. She tried to arch her back to loosen herself from him and move away, but she wasn't strong enough and couldn't make any more room between them. For the first time since she met him, she was scared.

Her words came quickly, 'What are you doing?'

'What do you see when you look at me?'

'What do you mean? Get off me. This isn't you.'

'It isn't? What do you see?'

She felt sick, bewildered by the change. 'I see you. I see my Jack.'

'You know me, right? You say you want me.'

Her voice steadied, 'I do. Let me up, Jack. I want you to let me up.'

He didn't. Jack laid his elbows down on the bed, their faces almost touching again.

He tightened his eyes, looked in pain. 'I wasn't... didn't mean to have feelings for you.'

'What? I don't understand, I...'

'Look at me. I said look at me. How did you escape?'

The seconds ticked past. She was sure he would be able to feel her heart pounding. Rebecca's eyes rolled to stare into space and thought back to that night many years ago. There was a lot she had blanked out, but recently it had been coming back to her. It was difficult but she thought hard. Eyes flashed in front of her. Suddenly she recognised them. *Jack's eyes!* It was Jacks eyes she'd seen in her dreams. He'd opened the door for her.

'I'm so sorry, Rebecca.'

When her eyes met his again they were wide with fear. Her body burst into action as she fought against him. She kicked out her legs, her back thumping the mattress over and over again.

'You... you were there.'

He struggled to control her. 'Calm down, STOP. I don't want to hurt you.'

Actions were repeated. 'GET OFF ME.'

Finally exhausted, her body fell still. They were panting together and their shared heat was making her uncomfortable.

Jack turned his head to whisper, 'Rebecca, I don't want to hurt you. I let you go - remember.'

She caught her breath. *Maybe if I relax he will let me up.*

'I didn't want to hurt anyone. It wasn't part of the plan. When you came home, disturbed us... the other's - they lost it. They didn't know you were there - until after.'

'Do they know you let me go?'

'No.'

He lifted himself carefully from the bed, allowing her to sit as he sat himself in a chair by the door.

She rubbed at her arms which stung from his grip.

I'm dreaming. 'This can't be happening. When we met... that could have been anyone. I could have been anyone.'

He shook his head.

'You were watching me.'

He nodded. 'For a while.'

'But you were put away.'

'I got out.'

'When?'

'Couple years ago.'

She was hesitant. 'They are still in jail?'

'No.'

'When?'

'Recently.'

She allowed herself to look at him. 'What am I doing here?'

'Listen, Rebecca...'

'WHAT AM I DOING HERE?'

He rubbed his head. 'It wasn't meant to happen. They weren't meant to kill anyone. If it wasn't for you, what you saw, they wouldn't have been sent down. Their lives were ruined in that place.'

Rebecca stood up. 'Their lives? What about my life, MINE? What about my parents lives?'

He stood to face her as she moved closer. She hit out - pounding her fists on his chest and arms. He let her at first but she tired quickly when the tears came. She let him hold her. His grip was tender again, just like the other times - safety.

'You're meant to babysit me for them aren't you? They want me dead too. Is that what's happening here? You're keeping me here for them.'

His voice struggled with the words, 'Yes. I don't want that though. I've grown to... I don't know. I, I think I-'

'Don't say it.'

'I want you to believe me.'

'Believe you? You've lied about everything - your work, losing your job.' She paused. 'Where's my phone, Jack?'

'I got rid of it. But listen, I didn't lie to you. You made presumptions about me. That wasn't my fault.'

'Don't! It was a lie, everything.'

He didn't argue with her again and they sat in silence for a long time.

*

It was early when she left for a walk, had left him asleep in the bed. Rebecca could have run, but she didn't. *Can't leave him now.* She felt exhausted, but she also felt she loved him back. She knew she was going to return to him. They'd spoken about leaving together.

In a way she was like him. She had nothing, not really. She'd abandoned her foster parents – not spoken to them for weeks. Without Jack she was alone. They were like two grains of sand on a beach with no ties to the world apart from each other. Now they could be together properly. *A fresh start.*

Rebecca thought it strange for the door to be ajar when she returned to the flat.

7. COMING OF AGE

Maren Schroeder

The morning after my husband's funeral I woke up with a stranger. I bolted from the bedroom and reached the kitchen as a memory of the previous day prodded awake the grief coiled tightly in my stomach. This was my first morning alone, without him.

I had been captivated by the play of light and shadow at daybreak for most of my painting life, but I was a night owl, not a lark. Rising early was tolerable only when Robert brought me to life. The malty aroma of freshly brewed coffee, in my favourite cup on the bedside table, teased me awake; his enthusiastic baritone in the shower; the buttery smell of freshly baked croissants pulled me from the warm oblivion of my dreams; the spicy scent of his aftershave lingered on the stairs – Rob had been the start of my day for more than thirty years. On the morning after his funeral our house was a stranger to me. Cold, sterile and silent.

The day before, I had been desperate to be alone. Dealing with my family's grief had left me no time or energy to deal with my own; I was close to breaking point. My son had noticed and with his father's charm and resolute manner called taxis, found coats and bags and walked our guests to the door, thanking them warmly for coming. Even Isobel and Elaine had agreed to leave. My girls had at first insisted on staying behind to tidy up, but Andrew had told them I needed space.

'I'll phone you tomorrow, Mum,' he had hugged me fiercely. 'Take care.'

He had closed the door behind him and I locked out the world.

I was never lonely at night. Padding through the house on silent feet, I would check on the children and my sleeping husband. Walk into my studio and consider the work I had done that day, and then, at last, settle in my red leather club chair with a book, content that the house contained all I needed in life. Last night, with no breath in the house but mine and trembling with fatigue, I went to bed without thought of anything other than sleep.

The morning after my husband's funeral the house was dark and empty. Robert was in every brick and lick of paint, the kitchen cupboards and living room shelves, but without his smiles and his warmth the house and I were strangers on the morning after a forgetful night – we couldn't bear to spend another moment together.

In Robert's office our answering machine started recording the first call of the day: 'Good morning, Mr Dowling, this is Carol from Creative Holidays...'

I grabbed my keys and left.

*

Six weeks after my husband's funeral, the GP called to say that the results for my tests had come back. Robert had insisted on them, for *his* sanity, he had said. It was Isobel's day to check in on me; she had answered the phone. I would have cancelled, I didn't want to see the doctor who had given Rob a clean bill of health the day before he died, but I was not in the mood for an argument with my daughter. Besides, I had to know.

'Good morning Mrs Dowling, how are you today?' the new receptionist asked, proud to have remembered my name. I wondered what she would say if I told her the truth.

'I'm fine, thank you,' was all I said.

'You're to go straight in; Doctor Miller's had a cancellation.'

At least I wouldn't have to sit and wait. I took a deep breath and knocked on Dr. Miller's door.

'Come in Helen, sit down. How are you keeping?'

'Getting there, I guess.'

Thanks to Isobel's skills my hair looked good today: freshly dyed, flyaway brown curls cut short for convenience. But the dark circles under my eyes, no make-up and a red wraparound dress no longer too tight gave him enough clues. I perched on the edge of the chair next to his. I would never tell him I spent the last six weeks avoiding the house, neither eating nor sleeping enough. Dr. Miller would want to discuss coping strategies and opening up to my feelings again. But losing control was too easy with my husband's shadow in every room. This morning a condolence letter from Joseph had come in the post and I had felt violently ill remembering how badly I had taken Robert's suggestion to visit him next year. That was our last fight, I wished–

Dr. Miller cleared his throat and looked up from my file: 'Well, the good news is that your memory loss isn't due to dementia. The bad news is your thyroid isn't working properly.' He flashed me a smile. 'You'll have to take medication and I'll refer you to a specialist for further treatment. You should be feeling better soon.'

'Thanks, Dr. Miller, good to know I'm not losing my marbles.'

My laugh was as shaky as my knees. I fell back into the chair and thanked him again. I had been so upset about my increasingly frequent lapses of memory, that Robert had begged me to stop obsessing about losing my mind and see the doctor instead. Since his death I hadn't worried so much, I felt the cloud threatening to descend on my mind had been lined with silver – I ached for oblivion. But now I wouldn't lose myself. I couldn't lose myself. Robert would have been so relieved – no, I flinched away from that thought. My grief was leashed tight; this was not the place to let it escape.

'Helen, I also want to prescribe you an anti-depressant. I know you didn't want it last time, but under the circumstances, I think it's advisable. Bereavement can make depression worse and I want you to take this just till your thyroid levels have normalised. It'll help you cope with things better.' Dr. Miller didn't hide his regret about Robert's death.

I couldn't hide the bitterness that rose in me like a hot flush. My spine stiffened and for the second time since I lost Robert, I welcomed a feeling other than sorrow. The ice cold lump of grief in my gut melted to rage until my heartbeat was roaring in my ears, drowning out his voice.

'Thank you,' I spat out and ground my teeth down hard on the words fighting to be set free. I snatched the prescription from his desk and ran out before I shouted at him that I didn't want to medicate my grief away; that my husband deserved better. Or that his incompetence had taken Robert from me. I stormed past the receptionist, her perfectly plucked eyebrows disappearing under a razor straight fringe, and barrelled through the heavy exit door into a morning clothed in winter greys.

Five minutes later I reached the Bean Street Café which had become my refuge in the last few weeks. I had never been there with Robert, there were no ghosts hiding in these walls.

'Good Morning, Helen, same as usual?'

'Just what I need, Trace, I'll be in the back.'

Tucked behind a lush potted bamboo and a tan leather sofa, my favourite table was free. The clatter of cups and plates on trays, shouted orders, and the occasional bubble of laughter over the murmur of the morning crowd soaked into me. A slow breath brought me the smell of oven warm cinnamon buns and the burnt chocolate aroma of roasting beans. I draped my jacket over the spare bistro chair and leaned back into the other. Tracey brought a steaming mug of black coffee to my table.

'I think this is the perfect boost for the kind of morning you look like,' she said, with an easy grin.

'Thanks Trace, I'm a bit shocked, I guess. The results for my tests are back, Dr Miller says I'm not going dotty, after all. I thought I was ready for anything, but it seems not.'

'Better than the other way round, don't you think?'

After a careful sip I said 'Yes,' then: 'How's business today?'

'Busier, the new girl is working out great and the weather is perfect: cold and dry.'

'I wish it was spring, I'm sick of the cold.'

'Coffee's nice and hot, that'll warm you up. Let me know if you want anything else,' Trace said and rushed to open the door for a guy in a smart coat who was struggling to get a double wide pushchair through the door. She was an incorrigible flirt, but her warmth and energy had made the Bean Street Café a haven for me.

The coffee swallowed the last of my anger. A low moan escaped my lips as I thought of my sudden exit from the surgery. Unwilling to examine my dramatic response to the GP's words, I looked around instead.

A picture-perfect blue-eyed baby boy with blonde curls was gazing at me and I smiled a silent 'hello'. At his excited chortle, his mother shifted him to her other shoulder and I was left staring at her French plait instead. Next to her, a woman with a gelled, straight-jacketed ponytail leant over and proclaimed:

'Must be terrible living with your husband's mother!'

French plait shook her head: 'Nah, she's great. Always sees what needs done, and she doesn't interfere, you know, it's much better than I expected.'

'Can't imagine living with *my* mother-in-law, she's a right bossy cow,' said the ponytail. 'Just as well you're getting some good use out of yours before she's completely crazy.'

'Nah, she's alright, but she's always there, you know, even when the kids are sleeping, and we –'

The woman with the baby whispered to the other and I turned away. My cheeks burnt and my jaw tensed as I imagined being discussed like this by my own family. I reached for a travel brochure from the magazine stand and stared at pictures of Italy in the winter. Robert again. I let out a loud breath, chose the local paper instead and started reading.

*

Seven months after my husband's funeral, I returned home from a visit to the travel agents' to find all three of my children sitting at the kitchen table.

'Well hello, how long have you been waiting for me?'

I could imagine what they wanted and even though I had expected it sooner, I wasn't looking forward to it. The kids weren't either, I thought. Isobel and Elaine looked into their cups and Andrew was looking at the door.

'Hi Mum.'

'Are you guys hungry? I'm starving.' I popped two slices of bread in the toaster and made myself a cup of tea.

'No thanks Mum,' Andrew said. 'We're here to talk to you about something.'

'The GP's office just phoned,' Elaine said. 'They said you could pick up your prescription tomorrow.'

'What's wrong with you?' Andrew sat up straight and looked at me for the first time.

'Underactive thyroid, nothing to worry about. Just have to take a few tablets.'

I spread blackcurrant jam on the toast and started to tidy the kitchen. Elaine walked over to me, took my plate and cup and set them down on the table: 'Please sit down, Mum.'

'It's just,' Andrew said, 'that we're worried about you, living here by yourself. Aren't you feeling lonely? The house is pretty big and, well, we've been wondering, since Dad passed–'

'We've noticed that you've been sleeping in the studio and we were wondering if you'd rather live with one of us. To be honest, Ricky and I would like to move in with you,' Elaine said. 'We had a long chat about it with Dad last year. Remember? We wanted to wait until he retired, but now...'

Now that Robert was dead, I thought, now that your father is dead you had no reason to wait.

'We'd need to discuss how it would work and things like that, but we really think it might be a good idea, Mum. What do you think?' Elaine licked her lips and turned her wedding ring over and over, waiting for my reaction.

I reached over the table and took her hand:

'It's alright, darling. I'm not upset with you.' I turned to Andrew and said: 'Get my bag from the hall please, would you?'

'Yes, Mum,' Andrew was quick to escape from the kitchen, but he returned just as quickly. I opened my bag and pulled out the folder I'd picked up in town.

'I think you and the boys living here is just what the house needs. I don't mind, but I don't want to be here when you do. I'll have a chat with you two later. If you can get it all done within two weeks, you guys can get settled in while I'm away next month.' I crossed my legs and picked up the folder to hide the trembling in my fingers.

Elaine glanced at her siblings, who both looked blank, then asked:

'Where– where are you going, Mum?'

'I'm going on that trip to Italy your dad was going to take me on for my sixtieth. And while I'm there, I'm going to visit an old friend in Florence.'

Andrew stared at me open-mouthed, Elaine gasped, and I felt like laughing for the first time since Robert died.

'But Mum…,' welled up from three throats and only Isobel clamped her mouth shut on the words. She looked at me with hazel eyes, the colour of her father's.

'Do you need any help booking flights, Mum?' she asked.

'Thanks darling, it's all arranged, but I need some new outfits for the trip. Do you want to come shopping with me?'

'Isobel!'

Isobel quelled her sister's complaint with a piercing look:

'I think this is a great idea. Italy is wonderful at this time of year and Daddy was always talking about how much he wanted you to paint in Tuscany. I can do next Saturday.'

I gave her a slow smile: 'Saturday is perfect.'

*

Eight months after my husband's funeral, our friend Joseph picked me up from the airport. I hadn't seen him for thirty-five years. He had sent family photographs occasionally, but I wasn't prepared for the difference between the memory of a long lost love and their sixty year old counterpart.

'You look great for an old man, Joe'

'You look— '

'Don't you dare say old woman to me, Joseph Carpenter!'

We found the easy companionship of our past within the first hour and I threw myself into exploring Florence. Having a personal tour guide was an effective antidote to the occasional painful wish to have Robert with me. But when we ventured into the shops along the Ponte Vecchio, I remembered his words again, about the River Arno and its bridges. Wherever we walked after that, I searched my memory for the times when Robert had shared his research with me, on the Medicis, the cathedrals and palaces, the artists and the many galleries. He had wanted me to paint the Piazza della Signoria with its statues, but I played a tourist instead, enjoying the sights.

On our last evening together, Joe asked me about my plans for the future.

'I haven't thought that far, yet, I've been concentrating on getting up each morning,' I replied.

'Will you start painting again? Robert sent me some photos of your new drawings in his letter last year.'

'Yes, I know, he told me…' *…and we had fought about it, no, I had fought about it. I hadn't wanted to get in touch with Joe and look like I was only doing so as an artist looking for a commission.*

'Well, are you still painting?'

'I – I don't know, I – maybe, when I get back.'

'Helen, Robert was so proud of your work; he would want you to paint again. Maybe it will help you bear his loss a little easier knowing that you are doing what he wanted you to.' Joe reached for my hand. I didn't pull away.

*

I returned to England feeling alive again. No doubt the thyroid tablets had helped shift the elephant which had been sitting on my shoulders for so long, but for the first time since Robert's death I had remembered the life we shared without flinching away from the memories. With my mind intact, denied the relief of forgetting, could I take on a future without Robert?

Elaine wanted to pick me up from the airport, but I took a taxi instead. Without an audience I wouldn't have to hide my reaction to the changes. Quick steps took me to the front door, keys jingled in my hands already, but the daffodils kept me outside. With clear eyes I looked at the house: a Georgian box with four rooms above, and four below, and a studio flat to the side where we had planned to live in our old age. A yellow sandstone front, evergreen ivy and a wisteria, sunlight reflected in the windows. The pungent earthy promise of a first warm day, the spirited tinkling of a goldfinch call and the sweet honey scent of daffodils coloured green the crisp spring morning. I drew a deep and easy breath and knew I had started to say goodbye not only to Robert on my trip to Tuscany, but to my old life, too.

I didn't know if I could stay here, in a granny flat, surpassed as mistress of my own house. But I did know that I wanted to paint again, and I would start with Rob's favourite view.

I went inside Elaine's house and waited for my family.

8. INFERIORITY COMPLEX

Chris Harris

-December 22nd, 2012
-Hemmingwell Asylum For The Mentally Different, Wellingborough, England

A bolt of lightning lit up the darkened room with an ear-splitting crack. Fork lightning was rare these days, but when it came, it certainly arrived with a bang. Just as it did tonight, announcing its sudden arrival by dethroning one of the stone gargoyles from its perch on the side of the titanic building. *Although, describing it as titanic doesn't really do justice to the majestic beauty of the original Titanic.* Instead, it was the sort of place where you would expect filming for a new Dracula movie to take place. *More menacing than majestic.* A gargantuan building, totally out of place amongst the district of smaller, seemingly insignificant rows of houses that surrounded it.

The cleaner, Jack, cursed as he stepped on one of the fragments of the dismembered gargoyle. As he peered down his weak eyes could barely see it in the darkness, which wasn't aided by the hazy effect that the pelting rain had on the landscape. The raindrops fell in quick succession, falling onto the uneven pavement before ricocheting off into oblivion. Jack, who had by now finished his shift, kicked the fragments to one side and walked away, whistling happily.

As he rounded the corner of the building he noticed a shadow just inside the main entranceway. He tutted furiously. *All patients should be locked away in their rooms at this hour.* He checked his watch quickly with an abrupt flick of his wrist. *Yes, far too late to be up and about.*

He pushed open the heavy wooden door, a feature he suspected the builders had only added to fit the horrific interior décor, none of which was clearly visible at this unsociable hour, with the entranceway lit by a solitary lamplight. It was in this faint beam of light that he saw a horror he will never forget.

Jack's eyes widened as he surveyed the scene, a choked gasp escaping from his throat. A headless corpse swung from a rope, tied by its ankles. On the bloodstained walls three words had been etched in spiky capitals 'NOT MY SUPERIOR'.

Jack recognised the faint blue/grey jacket that covered a white shirt. On closer inspection the name tag on his shirt confirmed that the headless corpse had once been Ross Wilson, the manager, if such a position could be called so in this place.

Jack stepped back, his heart pounding as he took his mobile phone out of his pocket, his shaking hands fumbling as he dialled 999. He held the phone to his ear and a long silence ensued before the phone beeped loudly. No signal. His loud curse echoed along the empty corridor. *Stupid bloody thing, just when I-* His thoughts were cut short as his panicked hands dropped the phone to the floor where it clattered noisily, the back cover coming loose and landing separate from the handset. He bent down to pick up the phone. He didn't hear the footsteps creeping up behind him, until it was too late.

*

Sex is rife in retirement homes, some say. These anonymous people also try to claim that sex is rife inside the Hemmingwell Asylum For The Mentally different. They are one hundred percent wrong. With over sixty of the one hundred or so patients in straitjackets for most of their time inside the facility and the other thirty-odd being either people with depression or some other sort of mental illness, such as Delusional Paranoia or Agoraphobia, the chances of any other patient, although inmate is another word frequently used, actually trusting another person to even speak with them properly was highly unlikely. Most the time, they didn't even know anyone else was there.

In all of its one year reign as the most 'efficient' asylum in England, it has had over five hundred patients, having cured many of them within only a couple of months. Of course, that involved a lot of psychiatrists working in shifts around the clock. Generally called 'quacks' by the patients, these were some of the best in the country and ranked somewhere in the world's top one hundred psychiatrists, a list most likely compiled by someone who has far too much time on their hands, who were themselves driven mad from compiling such a list.

Of course, this gruelling routine has its downsides. Psychiatrists here worked on eight hour shifts, morning, afternoon and night. The staff on the night shift were generally the worst and could probably pass for being patients themselves. Being deranged enough to come in between the hours of 10PM until 6AM, they were the only shift to actually diagnose and treat patients in their own cell room.

Controversy surrounded England's most famous Asylum. The statistics indicated that they had housed and treated five hundred and seventy five patients, yet fewer than four hundred have ever been accounted for. All evidence, what there was of it, showed no wrongdoings by the staff and all the patient attacks and murders had been accounted for. New security officers were soon put into place and they roamed the derelict hallways every night, watched by eyes that seemed to be there but were, in actual fact, just mere reflections of their torches off various minerals embedded into the stone walls. *Bricks were too easy for some of the stronger patients to remove.* They had never had a patient escape, even with the old security and there were very few incidents of violence inside the actual asylum walls.

The erecting of the asylum a year earlier also helped solve a problem in its surrounding area, the Hemmingwell estate. Notorious in its reputation for crime and gang violence, the County Council had built it as a prison. *A prison that would stare deep into criminal's blackened hearts and drive fear through them all.* It looked down on them all and, although not alive, the seamless nature of the exterior construct made it seem like it had grown out of the very earth itself. *And then there were the demonic gargoyles.*

Knowing that this prison was a threat, many gangs fled the area, relocating to other towns whilst swinging a false bravado about them to hide their darkest fears, which were realised by the building. And thus, the County Council had built a huge building, with no real use. The older prison was fine for now, but the previous asylum was falling to pieces.

So The Hemmingwell Asylum For The Mentally Different was born and it worked like clockwork, aside from the missing patients.

And the forgotten patient in block D...

*

Cell block D was currently out of use, but the cleaner was still required to clean there, in case a sudden of influx new patients necessitated its reopening. It was 10:30PM and, for now, it was in darkness and locked away behind a solid steel door, carefully hidden away from the outside world. There were two words scribbled hastily upon the door 'BOyLER ROoM'. These words fooled no one.

The secretive nature of Cell block D meant that even the bravest, or most deluded, patients kept well away. Rumours were a dangerous thing in a place where paranoid delusions were a common affliction, but still, rumours managed to emerge that there was something up there. Not a boiler room; the misspelling ensured that being a certainty. The rumours gave details of shrieking sounds every morning. A former cleaner, who was himself committed to the asylum due to the fact that he 'heard the ghosts', had gone into great detail about it, only to be dragged away, kicking and screaming by the brutal new guards. The new management, headed by Ross

Wilson, wasn't helping either, ignoring claims of the patients, dismissing them as delusions. The old management at least looked into the more sane claims.

*

The night cleaner, Matt, whistled softly to himself as he dragged his legs up the steel-rimmed stairs. He was heading towards the supply closet, located on the fourth floor. The same floor as Cell block D. He took out a heavy ring of keys, one for every cell in the asylum and every door, aside from the one that led to the 'BOyLER ROoM'. With a loud rattling of metal on metal, he found the right key for the cupboard door and pushed it into the lock and turned it. The lock gave a satisfying click. As he placed a hand on the cold, metal handle, he realising that something was disturbing him, a shiver trickled down his spine. *Weird.* He shrugged it off. The asylum was pretty creepy in itself, without the potentially dangerous patients. *But then, I knew that before I signed up to work here.* He had recently begun to doubt his own sanity at taking such a job.

He pulled a red Henry hoover from the cupboard, barely recognisable as most of the paint had chipped off over the last year. Its smile had been turned into two jagged fangs which stood out from the blood-red plastic that surrounded it. Searching for a plug, he noticed a door was ajar. He looked up at the heavy steel door. It said 'BOyLER ROoM'.

Now he knew what was worrying him. When he was on the morning shift, he had heard some of the things the previous cleaner had said about block D. The ghosts, the howling every night. Admittedly, Matt had heard strange sounds most nights, but had put it down to the wind or the piping around the exterior. He edged inside the room and saw, as he suspected, that the room was not a boiler room at all, but a room with strange symbols drawn on the walls in a red ink.

At least he hoped it was ink.

He prayed that it was ink.

Clank.

Footsteps. Matt turned, heart pounding. Something had escaped. Something deranged and perhaps dangerous. Something that was not on any records. Matt made for the door, thinking of hiding in the supply cupboard, but when he saw the shadow at the top stair he realised he had no chance of making it. *Only one way now, fight.* He bent down to the Henry hoover and dismantled the suction pipe, giving him a metal pole to defend himself with. He hid in the darkness of a corner near the door, the only thing giving him away was his shallow breathing.

Clang.

The heavy metal door swung shut and was locked from the outside. *The outside?*

Matt stepped out from his corner and yelled for help, hoping that the unknown assailant had a conscience, but all he heard was hurrying footsteps. Matt heard a noise and turned to see the resident emerge from the darkness at the back of the cell. He realised, as it drew closer, that he had no chance. Matt's hands shook violently. The thing reached out a hand; it held a thick, eight inch bladed knife, quite capable of easily carving through human flesh. Matt found he couldn't move.

The blade swung.

*

The exterior of the asylum was a basic rough cube, with five towers emerging from the main body of the vast building. The four towers located on the corners were designed to be watchtowers that overlooked the wide courtyard and each had floodlights on, which could easily be activated by the security room on the fourth floor at any time of need. The fifth tower was merely a clock tower, displaying a face not dissimilar to those on churches, and even appeared to be as worn. The large hand joined the small hand and the bells started to ring. Midnight struck.

The bells were loud and woke a few patients from their slumber, scattering the crows from the rooftops. Lightning struck again and the storm showed no signs of slowing. Instead it was gradually increasing in power, the bolts of lightning becoming more frequent. The rain kept coming too, hammering on the few windows of the building.

The large, minute hand moved forward ever so slightly, making it one minute past midnight. On the 23rd of December 2012.

The final day of the Mayan calendar.

One man, dressed completely in white, edged slowly out of the asylum doors and glanced up at the seemingly infinite amount of stone before the clock came into view. He sighed in what seemed relief and walked back inside. He believed, in the deepest, darkest pits of his mind, that the world was somehow going to end today. Today at 22:11.

But, here and now, at 00:01, known very clearly to this man, three people's world's had already ended. The man in white had left no evidence of his nonchalant walk.

Except a single footprint marked clearly in blood.

*

Block C was a psychiatrist's nightmare. This was the deranged and potentially dangerous ward, filled with those who had killed another, those who spent their waking days in straitjackets and their sleeping nights tied to the bed. Psychiatrists were not allowed to disturb them at night due to their potential, yet waning, danger and derangement. A guard patrolled this floor, a new one tonight, as the last one had mysteriously abandoned his post and his job. This one was bulky and towered around six and a half foot tall, much taller than most of the patients. He wore a uniform consisting of a white shirt, black trousers and a blue blazer with a name tag on. On his belt sat a ring of keys, a walkie-talkie, a truncheon and a Taser. He held a torch in his right hand, while his left remained fixed on the Taser's handle.

Jackson was on his very first patrol and throughout the shift, he felt like the other guards did not want him. They sneered at him. He felt before that he was no different to them, just wanting an easy job, but they quickly assigned him to the most dangerous floor and told him that they would be watching via the CCTV. *Maybe just an initiation. A test.* He shook his head and continued his cyclical walk around the block, the torch illuminating the way for him. He glanced around, pointing the torch in his line of vision. Nothing but concrete glared back at him. He turned the torch away. That was when he heard it.

Heavy breathing.

What was someone doing up here at this time? Is this a trick? Testing the new guy's bravery? The breathing was certainly close. Footsteps came from the stairwell. He twisted around, torch following his turn just in time to see a hem of white disappear up the stairs. He grabbed the walkie-talkie from his belt.

'Sec-Room. There is an intruder in block C, approaching block D. Am beginning pursuit. Over.'

He waited a second for a response. When there was none, he edged slowly and carefully up the stairs, not wanting to give the intruder any impression that he there. Pointing the torch downwards, he minimized the light escaping from his figure. With his free hand, he carefully slipped the Taser out of its holster, holding it in a ready position. He edged around the corner to see a white-clad figure fiddling with the lock on a door marked 'BOyLER ROoM'.

Suddenly his walkie-talkie bleeped. The guard tried to fiddle with it, but it was too late. The white-clad figure turned around, before a message from the security room came up.

'He's on the stairs. Over.'

Jackson stopped. Heart racing, he knew the message wasn't for him. *It was a warning for the other person.* The man in white turned and gave him a smile, before opening the door to the BOyLER ROoM and flinging it wide. Something stirred in the room's depths. Large, flat footsteps could be heard from inside, getting louder and louder.

Closer and closer.

Jackson aimed the Taser at the man's midriff. 'Stop this now,' he warned.

The man in white did nothing, so Jackson pulled the trigger on the taser. The man fell to the ground, shocked into unconsciousness.

The thing inside the room got closer to the doorway, but Jackson didn't let his shaking hands and rapid pulse distract him. He ran up to the door and grasped the handle, before slamming the door closed once more, a rush of adrenaline sweeping through his body. The key was still in the door, so he turned it in the lock, sealing it shut, before sliding it off the key chain and placing the rest in his pocket.

He sat on the stone floor and closed his eyes in relief and fear. *The others had given away my position. Threatened my life.* The unconscious man began to stir. Jackson knew he couldn't stay here, not with them knowing what he had done.

He had to run.

*

In Block B, Jared Gibbs slept with his pillow over his head, blocking out the sounds. The sounds could be any number of things from birdsong to whispers, but mostly they were bloody shrieks which formulated themselves into the never-welcome sound of a siren's scream. A scream that repulsed the mind, but attracted curiosity, one that you know you cannot resist, no matter how deep the terror takes hold.

Jared dared to resist.

Sometimes he could see blood drip from the ventilation duct in the ceiling. Only at night could he see it, the thick red substance oozing through the ceiling and pooling onto the floor with a drip as constant as the swinging of a pendulum, a metronome of death boring deep into Jared's mind and until only a hollow, twisted husk remained.

He never got the chance to show the pool of blood to anyone. He went down to breakfast, and by the time he returned, the pool was gone.

Jared Gibbs was delusional, they said. They said he was crazy, but he was sure that the cleaning cupboard was always ajar when he returned.

He knew that because he had once been the cleaner.

But he had seen the ghosts.

He was crazy.

Delusional.

9. SCARED TO DEATH

Aaron Mullins

The sight of the parrot filled her with dread. Cowering on the sofa, she clutched a cushion to her chest, flinching at every little flutter. Her eyes flicked between the parrot and the clock on the mantelpiece. *He'll be home soon. And that damn bird knows it.* The parrot turned to stare at her, its beady black eyes glinting with evil delight, as if it heard her thoughts and was eager to witness what was about to happen. *He's coming for you Meg.*

They stared at each other in silence. The ticking clock counting down every passing second.

Ten... nine... eight...

She realised she was clenching her teeth and eased the pressure on her jaw, releasing her breath in a long sigh. The parrot scratched against its wooden perch, an impatient, menacing sound that crept out of the cage and crawled into Meg's head.

Seven... six... five...

She snapped. 'Stop it,' she said, her fear cutting the sound to a shouted whisper. She glanced at the clock again. *Any minute now...* She knew what would happen when he got here. *His dinner's cooked, his clothes are clean, the house is tidy, but still...* There was always something. *Something not right, something out of place.* Always something.

She raised a hand to her breast, feeling the bruise where he'd punched her. *Overcooked the meat.* She reached up and pushed her fingers through her hair, wincing as they found the scabbed bruise on the crown of her head. *Forgot to clean his work boots.*

The parrot, bored of mocking its victim, lifted a wing and buried its head beneath it. Its body shook as it gnawed away at some unseen itch. *Filthy, flea-ridden creature. And Bill, what kind of name is that for a parrot?* It had been John's idea to get it, yet became her duty to feed it, to clean its cage. John had sat for hours teaching it to speak. *Can you say Meg's a whore? Over and over. Meg's a whore. Meg's a whore.* Eventually the bird had learned to copy its owner, so now every night she had to listen to the same words squawked at her by her caged abuser. *Meg's a whore. The only words that dumb animal had ever learned. Every. Night.*

Four... three... two...

Despite defiance, she felt a tear roll down her cheek. At least she was spared abuse during the day, from him and from the parrot. It never uttered a word when John wasn't around. *Only speaks on command of its master, showing off.* She quickly dried her cheek with the sleeve of her jumper. She hated giving John or the parrot the satisfaction of seeing her cry. Today she had more reason than normal to be upset though. There had been an accident. *Though he won't see it that way.* She had just finished replacing the water tube in the cage. *It wasn't my fault the stupid thing had tried to escape.* She knew what she had done as soon as she had closed the door. The feeling of soft feathered tissue and brittle bones crunching in a metal vice. The wild screeching and vicious grinding of beak on flesh as the parrot had torn at her hand.

She'd opened the door again instantly, allowing the parrot to fall back into the cage. But it was too late. The damage had already been inflicted. Bright green evidence had fallen gently onto the floor of the cage, supported by red that had oozed out of the pincer-like cuts on the back of her right hand. She'd hidden both. The green had found its way to the bottom of the rubbish bin, while the red was now disguised with a plaster. But still, he would know. *He always knows.*

The parrot had recovered from its ordeal. It had even spread its wings a couple of times since, though she was sure they didn't quite match now. A few feathers short on one side. She gripped the cushion again, her fingers digging into its cotton underbelly. *Jesus, he'll notice that.* She had thought about getting rid of the parrot altogether, saying it had died. But she knew the consequences of that would be even more severe. *It'd be my fault it died. I would be the killer.* She didn't dare think about what he would do to her then.

One... zero.

The parrot brought its head from beneath its wing, held still for a moment and then cocked it to one side. *It's listening. It can sense him.* She heard the jangle of keys inserted into the front door lock. The handle went down, followed by a long, high creak. Two heavy footsteps thudded into the house. He was home.

The slamming of the door fired off frantic activity in the cage as the parrot jumped and flapped its excitement at the return of its owner. Its injured wing seeming to flutter less vigorously, like a hypochondriac nursing a wounded arm. *So keen to tell the horrors of its day.*

The footsteps grew closer and John burst through the living room door. At the sight of him the parrot burst into song.

'Meg's a whore! Meg's a whore!' the bird shrieked with delight. Its greeting brought the usual idiotic grin to John's face.

'How's my little feathered friend' he asked, not even bothering to acknowledge Meg as he patted the lid of the cage.

She rose from the sofa, her eyes never leaving the floor as she made her way into the kitchen to fetch John's dinner. *Please God, don't notice.*

'What's the bitch been up to today then?' John asked.

'Meg's a whore!'

'Oh she is that alright,' John laughed.

'Meg's a whore!'

A moment of silence.

'MEG,' John yelled.

She froze. *Oh God, he's seen it. That damn parrot, he's seen it.*

'MEG,' John called again.

She looked down at the knife on the counter top, her heart racing. Her head ached, split decisions needing to be made. *Too late.* She felt a hand grip her left arm.

'When I call you, I expect you to answer,' said John, hot spit spraying her ear. A jolt of pain shot through her arm as he spun her round, his six foot seven build easily controlling her much smaller frame. She put her free arm up to protect her face.

'I'm sorry John, I-'

The blow crashed through her fragile hand and smashed into her cheekbone.

'You never learn, do you,' he said through a smirk.

She simply nodded in obedient silence. He released his grip on her and she breathed out.

'Fish pie?' he asked, the previous few seconds already forgotten, as if they were an irrelevant chore that he had to do whenever he came home, his duty to discipline his wife.

'Yes, with chips,' she replied, though he was already making his way back through to the living room. Relief flooded her body as she realised the reason for the attack was her hesitance. *He hasn't noticed. Thank God, he didn't see, thank you, thank you, thank-*

'Meg.'

'Yes John?'

'There's something wrong with Bill.'

***

Meg tested her weight on the leg. It hurt, but if she was careful she could walk. There was stiffness in the joints to go with the purpling bruises. She had never seen John so angry. His anger had quickly become her pain.

She wrapped her dressing gown around her and hobbled down the stairs. The packed lunch she'd made for John the night before was gone, as was his coat and work boots. She let herself relax a little. With a cup of tea in hand she settled onto the sofa. She could feel the parrot watching her. *Gloating.*

A bang on the door caused her to spill some tea on her robe. She patted down the excess, fearful not to spill any onto the sofa or carpet. She set the cup down on the table and made her way to the front door. Remembering what John had told her about people calling round, she cautiously called out to the unexpected visitor.

'Hello?'

'Good morning, would it be possible to speak with a Mrs Megan Brown?'

'Speaking.'

'Hello Mrs Brown. I'm Officer Clarke. I'm here with my colleague, Officer Wilson. May we come in to speak with you?'

'Police?'

'That's right Mrs Brown. Could you open the door please?'

She hesitated. *The police? John won't like this. But then he's not here, so I just won't tell him they were here. But what if someone else tells him? I could-*

'Mrs Brown?'

She turned the key and opened the door. She was greeted by the sight of two large men in police uniforms. They removed their helmets as one, the nearest spoke.

'Thank you Mrs Brown. May we come in?'

She stood aside and allowed them to enter. *He's not going to like this one bit.* She closed the door and turned the key before leading the officers through to the living room, trying her best to conceal the pain in her leg. She seated them on the sofa and lowered herself into the matching single-seater chair. She tucked her hands inside the sleeves of her dressing gown to hide their shaking. She knew the officers were staring at the purple blots of shame that flushed the side of her face. They shared a knowing glance before speaking.

'Mrs Brown. It's about your husband, John.' Officer Clarke began.

Oh Jesus, they know, the neighbours must have heard the screaming. He's going to be so mad! She could feel the trembling spread from her hands, along her arms and taking hold deep inside the pit of her stomach.

'I'm afraid there was an accident.' Officer Clarke continued.

Her eyes widened. A sickness had joined the trembling and her breath was coming in short, rapid gasps.

'A- an accident?' she muttered weakly.

'Yes, this morning. I'm very sorry Mrs Brown, but we are here to inform you that your husband John has been in a car accident and was pronounced dead at the scene.'

'Dead?' She repeated, the word barely audible even above the ticking clock in the otherwise silent room. The officer continued speaking; something about visiting the hospital to identify the body, but she was no longer listening.

'We'll arrange for a bereavement counsellor to come and visit. Do you have friends or relatives that we can contact for you in the meantime?' The officer asked, raising his voice a little to ensure he had her attention.

She shook her head. *Dead. Could it really be true? Was he really gone?* She'd wished for this day, for the release she wanted, but never had the strength to find.

'I'll be okay,' She eventually managed.

'Here's the number for the counsellor, a lovely lady. Please give her a call and arrange a time that's best for you.'

'I will. Thank you,' She accepted the card from the officer. 'If you don't mind, I'd like to be alone now.'

'Of course. If you need anything at all, then please don't hesitate to get in touch,' said Officer Clarke, rising from the sofa.

'I'm very sorry for your loss,' Officer Wilson added.

She flashed a half-hearted smile to the officers and quickly led them to the door. Once they were gone she returned to her spot on the sofa. She picked up her cup of tea, not caring now that remnants of her earlier spillage sat in a circular pool on the coffee table. *It doesn't matter anymore. Nothing matters now. He's not coming home. Not today, not ever again.* She didn't try to blink away the tears forming at the edge of her vision, she welcomed them. They weren't tears of sadness or pain, they were tears of relief and they were the last ones she would ever cry over John Brown.

***

Meg was dizzy. The events of the past few days had instilled a tiredness in her body which she longed to expel. There were very few family members to contact and no friends she thought would care. The funeral director had organised the rest. A short service followed by a long taxi ride home. *It was over.* Tomorrow she would begin to erase the unhappy memories. *Get rid of his stuff.* She didn't have any memories she wanted to keep, the torture of the past eleven years had tarnished them all. *A fresh start, that's what's needed.* The police counsellor had agreed. *Throw out his clothes, his belongings.* She glanced across the room.

'And it's goodbye to you too,' she called to the cage. There was no reply. With no master to greet, the bird had not uttered a word for the past nine days. She walked over to the silent creature.

'Nothing to say for yourself?' she shouted, shaking the top of the cage to get the bird's attention. For the first time she thought she saw fear in its usually cruel eyes. Satisfied, she returned to the sofa. *Think it might be time for another burial tomorrow. There's a nice spot in the back garden for you.*

The flustered parrot bowed its head in recognition of its fate.

Yes, tomorrow things would be different.

***

It hadn't taken her long to fall asleep, but she knew that it wasn't yet morning. The room was dark and her eyes struggled to adjust to the gloom. Something had pulled her out of her slumber. She reached over the bed and hit a button on her mobile phone. The sudden flash of light was painful, but squinting she could see that the time was 3:46am.

Then she heard it. The gentle ticking of a clock. She checked she was under a duvet and hadn't fallen asleep on the sofa. *There's no clock in here.*

The ticking disagreed.

She sat up, trying to work out where the sound was coming from. *So tired, must be dreaming.* The ticking appeared to have no origin that she could discern in her half-waking state. She lay her head back down on the pillow and tried to shut out the noise.

Ten... nine... eight...

From out of the darkness came the unmistakable jangling of keys. She bolted upright. She recognised that sound. It was one she'd waited to hear a thousand times before, the familiarity a stab of terror through her heart. *They're John's keys.*

The ticking was louder now, each second a thunderclap inside her head. *What the h-*

She tilted her head, straining to hear above the measured passing of time.

Seven... six... five...

She pulled her knees up to her chest and threw her arms around them. *Get a grip Meg. Get a-* She heard a long, high creak. *Oh Jesus, that's impossible.* Two heavy thuds from downstairs, a moment's silence, and then a slam that reverberated through the walls. The front door had been shut.

She shrunk back into the duvet, her body sliding down the headboard. Sickness was rising in her throat and she was gripped with a painful need to empty her bladder. *Maybe they'd made a mistake. Maybe John wasn't dead. Maybe he*

Footsteps passed by the bottom of the stairs.

Maybe it was John's idea of a joke. But I saw the body. Damn it I saw him, he was dead.

She heard the living room door open and a sound which chilled her body echoed up the stairs.

'Meg's a whore,' The parrot screeched.

But he's dead, I saw him...

'Meg's a whore.'

Oh Jesus, it is him! Meg was trembling uncontrollably now, her mind filling with images of the corpse she'd seen at the mortuary. Her imagination conjured undead visions of her husband returning from the grave where she'd buried him only the day before. And still the ticking grew louder, almost deafening now.

Four... three... two...

Meg ducked under the duvet and clasped her hands over her ears. The air quickly became sour from the heat of her breath. She closed her eyes. *Not happening, not happening.*

Footsteps were on the stairs now, heavy and slow, as if savouring the ascent.

She screamed, sucked in a lung full of stale air, then screamed again. Her hands grasped the side of her head, fingernails clawing at her scalp. The footsteps had reached the top of the stairs. She heard the handle of the bedroom door begin to turn. A dampness spread down her legs, her bladder released. She gagged as the sickness in her stomach lurched into her throat.

The bedroom door opened.

One... zero.

###

AUTHOR'S NOTES

This collection of short stories began life as a group of people from a writing forum deciding to publish their work together. I pulled it together as the editor and it turned into the anthology you see today. I made a few suggested changes to each story, but also wanted to keep the unique voice and writing style of each author. Could each story be more polished? Yes, certainly (can't all our stories!). But I also wanted it to be a reflection of the stage each author had reached with their craft, captured in time and telling their story, their way. The process of creating and publishing our work has helped us all grow as authors, and we are all proud of what we have achieved together. We hope you enjoyed it too.

ABOUT THE AUTHORS

AARON MULLINS

Aaron Mullins is an award winning, internationally published psychologist. Having studied creative writing at Northampton University, he started Birdtree Books Publishing where he worked as Editor-in-Chief. During this time he gained media recognition, partnered with World Reader Charity and sponsored English lessons in an under-tree school in India, before moving on to new ventures. He also taught academic writing at Coventry University. As a fiction author he's known for exploring the darker side of psychology in his work. He also creates business guides for entrepreneurs and writing guides for fellow authors. www.aaronmullins.com

ALAN PEABODY

Alan Peabody (also published as Anthony Preston) is a Northamptonshire based writer who has established himself professionally through writing thousands of words in the creation of expert reports to court in the course of IT litigation. This led to him contributing to the electronic evidence section in the Encyclopedia of IT Law. His works of technical fact and fiction have also been published in magazines. Alan gained recognition as runner up in the BBC Radio Write 06 competition. For Alan, creative writing is more than a hobby and less than a living.

STEPHEN TERRY

Stephen Terry is a semi-retired charity auditor, now living in Thailand. He writes full-time, mostly in the crime fiction genre. He has written for as long as he can remember. In later years he specialised in producing professional reports, from his reviews in over forty countries. His fiction writing has been well received and he has won a number of flash fiction competitions. In 2010, Stephen completed his first two full-length novels. The first, No Money No Honey, is a black-humour crime thriller based in Thailand. The second, A Date with Death, is a US based police detective thriller. In 2011 he produced two novellas, Hawaii High Five and Hawaii High Lo. All are available as eBooks from Amazon Kindle.

SOPHIE JONAS-HILL

A varied career as a jeweller, dressmaker, burlesque performer and confectioner, has left Sophie Jonas-Hill with little or no choice but to return to writing when she felt the need of an (early) mid-life crisis. She first began writing at the age of seven, when she published her early series of 'little chick' adventures on school issue note-paper. Despite assuring her careers teacher that she wanted to be an author and outlining the thirty seven novels she had written by the age of fourteen, she was distracted for the ensuing twenty-four years by life, love and the pursuit of, if not, happiness, then experiences, both good and bad. In 2011 Sophie decided to return to her first love, and began writing in earnest. She is currently working on her first novel, has three more in draft form, and a number of short stories.

KATE ROBINSON

Kate attended Aberystwyth University for 4 years, where she gained a law degree and post graduate diploma in legal practice. She spends her week days working as a paralegal and the rest of her time writing. She writes fantasy stories for young adults and hopes to provide stories that are a little different from the usual supernatural teen romance. She has a small orange cat called Mikho who is absolutely no help what so ever.

A G LYTTLE

A graduate of Queen's and Surrey, A G Lyttle has published a number of short stories and articles. He is currently polishing up his first novel, Starlings in the Corn, about Nick McQuaid, a young Protestant growing up in sixties Ulster and battling to break free from a background of poverty – with a little help from the IRA. It will be the first book of a trilogy. The short story presented here was inspired by a visit to one of the more obscure tourist attractions in his favourite European city. Home to musicians, artist and literary savants through the centuries, Paris also boasts an underground ossuary that displays the bones of over six million of its former citizens.

ANGELA KELMAN

Angela Kelman lives with her family in Aberdeen, Scotland. It was here where she studied and achieved her diploma in Photography. She started writing seriously about two and a half years ago after being propelled into, what some people call, 'free time and coffee' - after her youngest of two boys began nursery. Angela writes short stories and in 2011 won August's competition on Writers billboard. She is now actively seeking publication for her first Young Adult/Fantasy Novel, The Kylo. As well as novels and short stories, Angela enjoys writing poetry - you can see examples of her work along with the blurbs for her novels on her website, available in the author contact section.

MAREN SCHROEDER

Born in East Germany, Maren Schroeder studied English and Journalism at Leipzig University. After longingly peeping through the Iron Curtain throughout a childhood filled with adventure stories and patriotic poems, Maren set off to explore Scott's Scotland in 1994. She went to Edinburgh University for an exchange year, but fell in love with Scotland (and a Scotsman) and decided to come back after finishing her degree. Now lost in Fife, she fills her days with reading, writing and baking experiments. With three hungry boys, an open-minded husband and cake-loving friends she has guinea pigs galore, but feels the time has come to send her stories into the wild.

CHRIS HARRIS

Chris Harris is a science-fiction/fantasy author who occasionally dabbles in horror. He is a student from England and his first novel, The Four Swords: Xaos 1 placed in the top twenty best-sellers in science fiction on Amazon. His second book, The Lords: Xaos 2, is due to be published early spring 2012.

38756143R00052

Printed in Poland
by Amazon Fulfillment
Poland Sp. z o.o., Wrocław